Ursula Dorn

I was a Wolf Kid from Königsberg

Biographical novel

Commented by PD Dr. Winfrid Halder

Ursula Dorn

Ich war ein
Wolfskind
aus Königsberg

Biographischer Roman

Mit einem Kommentar von PD Dr. Winfrid Halder
Direktor der Stiftung Gerhart-Hauptmann-Haus,
Deutsch-osteuropäisches Forum, Düsseldorf

edition
riedenburg

*For my son Klaus
and my granddaughter Janina*

Bibliographic information of the German National Library:
The German National Library lists this publication in the
German National Bibliography; detailed bibliographic data is available
on the internet via https://www.dnb.de/EN/Home/home_node.html .

Notification

Thanksgiving

Author, publisher and reader thank PD Dr. Winfrid Halder for his comprehensive and
many-faceted commentary.

In memory of Prof. Dr. Horst-Peter Hesse who made possible the initial contact with
the author

2nd englisch edition	July 2019
© 2019	Ausbildungs- und Forschungszentrum ETHNOS e. V.
Office	AFZ ETHNOS, Bermesdickerstr. 9, 44357 Dortmund
Internet	www.afz-ethnos.org
E-Mail	afz.ethnos@gmail.com
Translation	Dr. Walther Friesen
Typesetting and layout	Tatiana Friesen
Publishing house	BoD – Books on Demand, Norderstedt

ISBN 978-3-74-942920-2

Table of contents

The burden of memory

Prologue

In the year one thousand nine hundred and ninety-two

Brief an den Präsidenten der Litauischen Republik, Vytautas Landsbergis, am 5. Februar 1992

Sehr geehrter Herr Präsident!
Sie werden sicher erstaunt sein, von einer einfachen Frau aus dem Land Deutschland Post zu bekommen. Aber ich musste es einfach aus meinem Herzen heraus tun.
Hier ist kurz mein Vorleben!
Ich bin 1935 in Königsberg, dem heutigen Kaliningrad, geboren und habe den schrecklichen Krieg 1945 voll miterlebt, war dann 10 Jahre alt. Nach 1945 trat die schwerste Zeit meines jungen Lebens an. Mein Vater war Soldat in Russland und ist bis heute noch als vermisst gemeldet. Meine Mutter hatte 5 Kinder, das älteste war ich. In der Zeit von April 1945 bis Ende 1946 waren 2 dann verhungert, und ich habe mich als 10-jähriges Kind in einen russischen Munitionstransportzug, der bei Nacht und Nebel per Bahn nach Russland über Kanas/Litauen fuhr, reingeschmuggelt und bin dann so auf dem Bahnhof von Kanas in Litauen gelandet. Nun stand ich mutterseelenallein da in einer total fremden Welt für mich. Ich machte mich fortan auf den Weg in ungewisse Etwas. Ich musste feststellen, dass die Leute alle so gut waren und mir immer überall, wo ich hinkam immer zu Essen und Trinken gaben. Auf diese Weise habe ich bis Oktober 1948 ihr Land und Leute als Kinder-Bettlerin und jeden Tag eine Strecke von bis zu 20 Kilometern und mehr kennen- und liebengelernt. Habe auch große Gefahren überstehen müssen, wenn sich in manchen Ortschaften und Wäldern nachts Partisanenkämpfe abgespielt haben und ihre Landsleute und kleine Bauern im Land ermordet wurden, bei denen ich manchmal nachts Quartier bekommen hatte. Es waren für mich furchtbare Augenblicke, die ich bis heute nicht vergessen kann. So wie die Erlebnisse in Königsberg. 1948 wurde ich dann mit vielen, vielen Tausenden deutscher Kinder von den russischen Besetzern in LKW's nach Kanas transportiert, die sie überall im Land aufgesammelt hatten und zum größten Teil elternlos waren. Von dort aus wurden wir dann registriert und dachten, es geht ab nach Sibirien, aber es war anders. Wir wurden über Königsberg und Polen in verblombten Güterzügen nach Eisenach/Thüringen in die ehemalige DDR gebracht. Wurden dann nach 5 Wochen Quarantäne im Land aufgeteilt. Ich bin dann noch 5 Jahre in der damaligen DDR gewesen und habe da die Schule besucht. Konnte überhaupt kein Deutsch mehr, sondern nur etwas russisch und perfekt Litauisch. Es war sehr schwer für mich, habe sehr fleissig geübt und gelernt, auch noch einen Beruf erlernt und bin dann 1953 in den westlichen Teil von Deutschland geflüchtet über Berlin.
Seit dieser Zeit lebe ich hier und bin verheiratet sowie berufstätig und habe einen Sohn, der es weitaus besser hat als wie es mir ergangen ist.
Nun, Herr Präsident, es war weitaus viel mehr, aber das war die Kurzfassung.
Nun zum eigentlichen Brief: Ich möchte, und das ist mein sehnlichster Wunsch im Sinne bestimmt vieler tausender, heute erwachsener, deutscher Menschen, die das gleiche schwere Schicksal in ihrem Lande erlebten und von den liebevollen, freundlichen litauischen, gastfreundlichen Menschen praktisch vor dem Tod gerettet wurden, ein großes Dankeschön aussprechen. Und bitte geben Sie das auch mal ganz öffentlich im Fernsehen bekannt, damit das auch all ihre Landsleute mal erfahren, was die alle Gutes an unseren Kindern nach 1945 getan haben. Danke, Danke, Danke.
Hiermit habe ich mir, was mir schon lange im Herzen lag, runtergeschrieben. Auch möchte ich mal sehr gerne wieder ihr Land besuchen, das wäre ein großer Herzenswunsch von mir. Es ist für mich, bei aller Liebe zu Königsberg, mehr Heimat geworden als mein Geburtsort.
Nun hoffe ich, Herr Präsident, dass Sie diesen für mich wertvollen Brief auch lesen dürfen und ihn auch veröffentlichen. Vielleicht schreiben Sie mir auch mal, dass ich weiß, ob der Brief angekommen ist.
Es grüßt Sie und ihre lieben Landsleute von ganzem Herzen ihre *Ursula Dora*

vielen Dank!

LIETUVOS RESPUBLIKOS AUKŠČIAUSIOJI TARYBA
SUPREME COUNCIL OF THE REPUBLIČ OF LITHUANIA
OFFICE OF THE PRESIDENT

Vilnius, den 19 März 1992

Sehr verehrte Frau Ursula Dorn,

Im Namen des Präsidenten des Obersten Rates der Republik Litauen, Vytautas Landsbergis, möchte ich mich bei Ihnen fur Ihre Schreiben und Ihre Interesse an Litauen, bedanken.

Wir antworten auf Ihren Brief von 5. Februar 1992 und teilen mit, dass wir uns mit Ihren Brief aufmerksam bekanntgemacht haben.

Wir werden Ihren Brief in die unsere staattliche Zeitung "Lietuvos aidas" bringen und drucken lassen.

Mit grosser Herzlichkeit möchte ich bei Ihnen fur Ihre Hochachtung gegenuber dem litauschen Volk Dankeschön sagen.

Mit freundlichen Grüssen

Asta Bogušienė
Sekretärin fur Aussenkorrespondenz

Letter to the President of the Lithuanian Republic, Vytautas Landsbergis, on February 5, 1992

Dear Mr. President!

You will surely be amazed to receive a mail from a simple woman from the country of Germany. But my heartfelt desire has urged me to do it.

Here is my previous life!

I was born in 1935 in Königsberg, today Kaliningrad, and I fully experienced the terrible war in 1945, when I was 10 years old. After 1945, the hardest time of my young life began. My father was a soldier in Russia and is still reported missing. My mother had 5 children, I was the oldest one. In the period from April 1945 to the end of 1946, 2 of them starved to death, and I, a ten year-old-child, smuggled myself into a Russian ammunition transport train, which went in the dead of night to Russia via Kaunas / Lithuania and so I landed at the Kaunas railway station in Lithuania. Now I stood there all alone in a totally strange world for me. I made my way to uncertain something. I realized that the people were all so good and always gave me food and drink wherever I went. In this way, until October 1948, I, as a child beggar, got to know and love your country and people, covering every day a distance of up to 20 kilometers and more. I also had to endure great dangers, when partisan battles took place at night in some places and forests and your compatriots and small peasants were murdered in the country at places, where I sometimes got shelter for the night. Those were terrible moments for me that I cannot forget until today. Like the experiences in Königsberg. In 1948, with many, many thousands of German children, I was transported by truck to Kaunas by the Russian occupants who had picked them up all over the country and for the most part they were without parents. We were registered there and thought, it would go off to Siberia, but it was different. We were brought over Königsberg and Poland in sealed freight trains to Eisenach / Thuringia in the former GDR. We were then after 5 weeks quarantine distributed throughout the country. I was then still 5 years in the former GDR and attended school there. Could not speak German at all, but only a little bit Russian and perfect Lithuanian. It was very hard for me, I trained and learned very hard, mastered a profession and then, in 1953, I fled to the western part of Germany via Berlin.

Since then, I live here; I am married and employed and have a son who is much better off than I had to experience.

Well, Mr. President, there were a lot more, but that was the outline. Now to the actual letter: I would like, and that is my dearest wish – surely also in the sense of many thousands, today adult German people who had experienced the same heavy fate in your country – to convey the heartfelt thanks to the friendly, hospitable Lithuanians who had practically saved them from death.

And please also announce it publicly on television, so that all your people will know about the good things they have done to our children after 1945.

Many thanks to you again and yet again.

Hereby I have written down what has been already in my heart. Also I would like to visit your country again, that would be my dearest wish. For me, with all my love for Königsberg, it has become more home than my birthplace.

Now I hope, Mr. President, that you will be able to read this letter, which is valuable to me, and also to publish it. Maybe you will write me once in a while so that I knew if the letter has reached you.

You and your dear compatriots greets with all her heart.

Ursula Dorn, Many thanks

Vilnius, 19 March 1992

Dear Mrs. Ursula Dorn,

On behalf of the President of the Supreme Council of the Republic of Lithuania, Vytautas Landsbergis, I would like to thank you for your letter and your interest in Lithuania. We respond to your letter dated from 5 February 1992 and inform you that we have acquainted ourselves with your letter.

We will forward your letter to our state newspaper "Lietuvos aidas" to have it printed.

With great cordiality I would like to thank you for your respect for the Lithuanian people.

Yours sincerely

Asta Bogušienė
Secretary for Foreign Correspondence

Backgrounds: Wolf Kids

Introduction by Heike Wolter (Editing)

Wolf Kids

After the turmoil of the Second World War, German children tramped like hungry wolves through Poland and Lithuania to stay alive or to find the bare essentials for their families during their begging jaunts. A sheltered childhood was not their lot. Misery and fear shaped the development of these children.

It was not uncommon that at the end of the Second World War, after the Soviet troops had occupied East Prussia in 1945, children couldn't find their families again; their parents were starved to death, expelled from their homeland or killed. So they were on their own.

The historical research assumes that there were about 25,000 such children who trekked alone or in small groups across the country. About 5,000 of them managed to flee to Lithuania. They were mostly supplied by Lithuanians for some time there. But only small children who had quickly adapted to their new lives, learnt Lithuanian and forgot their German background remained permanently in the families. All the others, after having been admitted for a while but also used as cheap labor, were sent on. That might have been mainly the case because the Luthunians themselves were in need and they had fear of being captured on the spot by the Soviet military. Then their families were actually in danger of being deported.

Many wolf kids had lost their lives during their treks – having died of starvation, exhaustion or had been battered to death. Others stayed in Lithuania, forging a new identity there. Still others – about 200 – resettled in Germany. Oftentimes with the life motto: 'Be glad that you live; forget what was; look straight ahead!'

Only cautiously they are now looking for the vestiges of their identity. But looking back might be helpful to this 'forgotten generation' (Sabine Bode*) that stood between all frontlines.

The author, Mrs. Dorn, has recognized this when she writes that she has 'committed herself fully to paper' with this book.

Sabine Bode. Die vergessene Generation – Die Kriegskinder brechen ihr Schweigen. 20. Auflage. Klett-Cotta, Stuttgart 2014, ISBN 978-3-608-94797-7.

I was a Wolf Kid from Königsberg

Biographic novel by Ursula Dorn

Where I come from

My parents were Asta Wedigkeit, born Hauke, and Franz Wedigkeit. My mother was the twelfth child of her parents Irma and Gustav Hauke. They were self-reliant shipmen, and my mother married my father Franz on 13 April 1935 in Königsberg.

I was born on 19 April 1935, also in Königsberg. Four more siblings came also after me. One sister and three brothers. I grew up on a barge of my grandparents until I was six, because my parents were also on the boat at that time. As I went to school, my parents rented an apartment in Königsberg. We lived in Unterhaberberg. There was also a school nearby that I went to until I was almost ten years old. In between, we moved again. To the city center, Vorstädtische-Langgasse 139. My grandmother Irma also moved then to the city, because my grandfather had died in the meantime, and her sons took over the two barges. Grandma Irma moved to the Kontiner Way, and there was also a small garden with a cabin in which she wanted to live alone.

We children were very happy to be able to travel to our granny, now and then. I often travelled by tram that stopped right at our doorstep. I went then to Grandma without paying. Quite often, I also stayed there overnight and went to school from there, but always without money. The conductors knew me already and always smiled when I sat there. My granny received only a small pension and wasn't able always to gift us some money. Yet, we were overjoyed to get a coin from her and then went to buy some candies. Granny had several berry bushes in the garden, and we always plundered them plain in summer. Everything that grew there was just to our liking.

In 1939, my father was called up for military service and straightway transported to France, together with many other men who had to leave their young families alone. No one suspected that with this the great suffering for all would begin. Also for my mother with her four children at that time kicked it off. It was flat and skinny without the family's breadwinner although my father hadn't been earning a lot of money. He also came from a child-rich family with eight other siblings. Everyone had just only the bare necessities there.

In any case, we children missed our father very much and I especially, because I was very attached to him. I was always able to talk with father very well. He also often took my brother Herbert and me on land trips with the truck, when he had to supply the bakers with flour or to bring flour from the mills situated not very far from Königsberg to replenish the silos at the Pregel. We were overjoyed, if we were allowed to travel with. But that was all past for us. The father was gone, and we all grieved for him. From time to time, a letter came from the front to us, and so we received at least a sign of life from him. A leave was not to be hoped for, but one day something very special came. He sent a package from France to us with a superduper chocolate and some other sweets, and there were also two beautiful dresses in it, all in white for my little sister Eva and me. They looked so beautiful, and we were very proud of them. My brothers Herbert and Hans received two small wooden cars. Our joy was great, but we were still missing our father badly.

Children's world in Königsberg?

The times were getting worse and worse. And over time, the Russian army began the military airstrikes on our city, and one had always to be on the alert being out in the street. The attacks of the war planes with on-board weapons were the most dangerous. They came down flying low over the rooftops all along. It was very bad.

Food supplies were also getting worse for all of us. All

commodities, such as butter, sugar, flour, and bread could only be obtained with ration stamps. Fruit couldn't be thought about at all. It was also impossible to procure clothes and if any, then only with procurement certificates. It was really awful already. I had barely a pair of shoes to wear. A man from the district administration also came often to us and prompted my mother to leave the city, as quickly as possible. We were preferred because we were a family with many children; but my mother was stubborn and didn't think about leaving Königsberg. If she had done it, we all could have been spared a great deal of harm that was approaching us.

We children viewed our world with much saddness. We almost didn't play anymore, outside we couldn't because of the grenade strikes, and so we turned automatically into cellar children who barely surfaced to take an airing. Once I was terribly lucky. A large military car stopped at our front door; it had been loaded to the brim with shoes. I grasped the fortunate situation and asked a soldier for a pair of shoes for me and my siblings. He said, "Go up and pick out some for you". I rummaged around until I found about my size and also snapped some shoes for my siblings about the sizes that could probably fit them. They were all tied up with laces. I gave thanks for this and ran up to my mother with full arms; she was really amazed at what I was dragging along. And a large-scale trying on kicked then off. They didn't fit back and forth, but we wore them, even if there were bubbles on our heels afterwards.

With the school it was now more and more downhill because of many air attacks. There was a lesson once in a while and then again not. Often, when the alarm sirens were howling, we had to wait for the end of the airstrikes in the school air shelters. Then there was screaming of kids down there.

One day, it was all over, and we were not allowed to go to school anymore. I couldn't understand why I couldn't go there anymore and sneaked away secretly from home just to see if it was open again.

Small Getaways

Sometimes, when it was quiet in the streets, I ran then quickly to my aunt Agnes who lived only a few blocks further away; she was my mother's older sister. I always felt very comfortable there. It was always so cozy there. We had then a nice breakfast with her daughter Karin who was 16 years old, and some stories were told us; I had never experienced it with my mother. I don't know why, but she never did anything like that with us kids. I also watched how Agnes sewed with the sewing machine when she tailored something for her daughter. I took a great interest in all that. What became too small for Karin was then given to me and my little sister. It was then changed by Aunt Agnes. We were happy about those beautiful things.

At home, it didn't look so rosy, that's to say. My mother was also a strong smoker, and even our butter ration stamps were exchanged to get some smoking material. Since I was the older daughter, I always had to go to the neighbours and exchange the stamps. Thus, the children were also deprived of what they really deserved. That's why Aunt Agnes and my mother often had clashes. She couldn't understand it at all.

She then also got to know a woman friend called Sahm; and then they often went away and so we stayed during the air attacks under difficult conditions in the basement or remained in our apartment. I always had to take care of children, because I was the older one, but I also was terribly afraid that something could happen to us.

Then my mother met a soldier. He and others had been deployed as a unit on the grounds of our community garden. We had a beautiful large summerhouse; before the air raids we had been often staying there in summer to enjoy the weekends. But then it wasn't possible anymore. If it was stilly over the city, we dared to get out, but that was rarely the case. Only my mother went quite often there, now because of her boyfriend. My little step-brother Max was born from this relationship. For my father, who hadn't been home for a long time and one day came on vacation, probably the whole world collapsed when he saw the child. I remember exactly the look on his face. This was followed by a terrible marriage crash between father and mother; we couldn't understand at all what was going on and had to witness everything, full of great fear. We all cried terribly, and then my father went away and didn't come back for a few days, even though we didn't stop asking, "Where's our dad?" But he didn't come home. Then suddenly he stood before us. We all hung on dad. Everyone had the right to sit with him on his lap and caress him. I think he also enjoyed being hugged by all his children. Only for the youngest there was no feeling. He wasn't even really taken care of, but we kids all loved and spoiled him. Our father stayed a few more days with us, but then he had to leave again. We were all very sad about it and would have liked to have him with us.

Now my father was transferred to Russia with his unit, and no one knew for how long. How could it have been between my parents? Goodbye! We couldn't realize it to the full extent, after all the disappointment our father had.

In The War

Our games on the road were getting more and more dangerous for us, from day to day. Yet, we managed sometimes to get to the community garden of our grandma Irma and then slept there, when it was too dangerous for us to go back home. And the trams didn't run regularly already because of the airstrikes. Somehow, we always managed to get back and forth.

Many sailors coming from the central railway station passed almost daily by Kontiner Weg, where Grandma had a garden; they went to the Schichau shipyard at the port, where they had to report for duty on warships. Then we had fun asking them if we could carry their belongings along for a little while. They usually laughed at us and gave us something to carry. For that we also got some money or candies, and we were beaming with joy. Because soldiers were well provided with everything. But we always had to watch out because of the Russians' low-flying aircrafts. Once we had to stay with grandma and did not manage to get to the air shelter bunker that was very close to the garden.

My brother Herbert as well as my brother Hans, Grandma and I had to lie on the floor, which we had previously laid out with some blankets. We were all scared. Then later we fell asleep from fatigue. In doing so, we didn't notice at all that the left ear of my brother Hans had been gnawed at away durung the night. In the morning he was lying there wholly smeared in blood and no one knew what it was. Then my grandma said that it might have been a rat, and all of us got suddenly really scared.

Wood and coal were also getting scarcer, and then we went to the goods train station, adjacent to our community garden, where coal wagons were stationed sometimes. We got covertly some pieces of coal out of the wagons down, but that had to go lightning fast, because there were always railway watchmen running around. But we were quite smart in organizing it and always had luck. Sometimes we also played on the rails between the wagons. It was very dangerous, but we had great fun. An uncle of mine sailed always his boat to the Schichau shipyards to fish out with a hand net some pieces of coal from the harbour basin. Now and then I also went with. Then we got a share of it. And so we were keeping ourselves above water.

Then my grandma Irma moved into the apartment of her daughter Agnes, because the airstrikes became stronger and stronger now, and she couldn't stay alone in the community garden. We had already had a great attack behind us and, I guess so, those had been the Englishmen. Within two hours they had managed to reduce the whole city center to rubble; the bombing was started at about two o'clock at night. It was terrible. The sirens went off; everyone was torn out of sleep. Everyone milled around in the streets. There was no order at all. People looked up to the bright sky; it glittered all up in the air because of tinfoil pieces, which had been previously thrown from the aircrafts. They had formed a huge cross that spread in the air across the city center, and we all ran for our lives. We managed only just in time to get to the air raid shelter at Oberhaberberg (Central railway station). I'll never forget it. Because of the high pressure wave from the bomb blast, all the people in the bunker fell over. I broke outright down with fear and thought, we were all dead now. There followed a series of strikes without end, and the whole city was on fire. But no one could help.

The bombardment had eased by morning, and some brave people began slowly to leave the bunker. We were still full of fear in the body and didn't dare to come out. Also, for the simple reason that the all-clear signal hadn't been given yet. Then suddenly we saw our aunt Agnes with her daughter Karin and Grandma, all chalk white in the face out of sheer fear. They were totally weirded out to see us here. They had come in at the other end of the bunker, and since everything was dark, we couldn't see each other before. Now we made the decision and, like all other people, took ourselves outside. It was terrible, everything was burning, and everyone was groping his way in the streets as far as it was possible. We were incredibly lucky. The house we lived in had remained safe. Aunt Agnes was very much excited; we had to go with her and see, if her apartment in the Knochenstraße had been left intact. But we saw from a distance that all the houses were in rubble and ashes. We all broke into tears and clamped together with despair.

Now the three didn't have their home anymore. Everything was gone; they had only their bare lives. They stayed with us for the first time, until everything more or less calmed down. Aunt Agnes then tried to find another apartment, and it didn't take long, then one in Unterhaberberg was assigned to her. They were extremely happy about it, because it was too much for us with so many people in our not-too-large apartment and then mostly together in the air-raid shelter. The relatives gathered up everything what was left to make it somewhat homely for them.

Life in the dark

From then on, it was even difficult to walk around the streets. The shelling from the planes with on-board weapons occurred now many times a day and that was always in low-level flights. People always ran close to the walls of houses. If I wanted to go to the bakery over the way, then I had to watch out all along not to be hit by a shot. There was no escape from them anywhere in the city now.

Our living played out almost exclusively in the air-raid shelter, because the sirens didn't manage any longer to warn the people. Once we were up in the apartment (4th floor), as my mother eventually wanted to try to cook a decent lunch for all of us. She had managed to get something from the butcher the day before. There had to be goulash, and we were very much looking forward to it. By the time we were up in our apartment, we heard a terrible bang, and we all fell down onto the floor. It was a Stalin's organ that had hit the house next to us. Our house had also got a part of it, all the windows were broken, doors flew up, and some pieces of furniture turned over. We all lay on the floor frightened to death, and no longer dared to get up. My mother cried out then loud "All get up and quickly off to the cellar!". We all raced down to the stairwell. There were shards all over.

As we got down, all other housemates sat around, as white as a sheet in their usual corners. At first my mother didn't go upstairs from sheer fear. Later on, we went upstairs to see what all the damage was. It was not much left of the furniture. We sorted out what could be saved. The windows were nailed with cardboard, because it was still icy cold outside. To start with, we had to bring it from the basement rooms, which couldn't be used now for living, anyway. The cellar had turned into our main dwelling place.

In spring, all of us children had got whooping cough. That was terrible, and it took weeks, till we got some kind of relief. There was no medical help for us, because nobody wanted now to get out running the risk of being shot at. The hospitals were full of wounded soldiers, so there was no place for civilians anymore. In addition to that, my youngest brother got pneumonia. Now we had no rest day and night, one of us was always coughing. My mother had to do with Max, and I helped the elder brothers during the bouts of illness, at moments, also my little sister Eva. If possible, we took ourselves off to open basement shafts to get a bit of fresh air.

Our housemates helped us as well, if that was possible.

Our youngest brother didn't survive it. He was only nine months old and died one morning at 10 o'clock. It was very bad for all of us. He was then buried in the Ponather cemetery under very difficult circumstances. Only my mother could still go there all alone. It could be too dangerous for us to be there with her.

Bit by bit, our whooping cough was over, but we all were even more weakened than before. We were lacking the necessary food. The school had been completely closed for weeks now, because the bombardments in and outside the city became stronger day by day. Everything was getting more and more frantic. People from the neighbourhood, whose houses had been already broken, always came over to our air-raid shelter, and they all lived only provisionally in it. But we had been still lucky till then.

One day, a few young soldiers aged not older than 14, 15 years came into our cellar for the street defence; they placed themselves on some wooden boxes in front of the cellar shafts with the view out to the street. They had decided to fire at the Russian enemy in this way. That's what we had been told. The people in the shelter disapproved of it and couldn't believe that almost half children had been summoned up for this purpose. The military clothing and the coats they wore were so long that they dragged the whole uniform junk behind them.

Stay or leave?

It was getting worse from day to day, and now some people came constantly to my mother and said, "Mrs. Wedigkeit, you have to get out of Königsberg with your children! It's not much time left for you anymore. There are still a few ships heading towards Denmark across the Baltic Sea with wounded soldiers. A few children-rich families can still come with." But my mother couldn't be persuaded to make it happen.

Why? I've never understood because she had to think of her four children still alive. Although her sister Agnes and also Grandma Irma repeatedly said, "Asta, take your children away!", it didn't help. She didn't do that. She said to an official, "you can put the gun on my chest. I'll stay here!" For all of us, it was madness to think so.

Then, just before the approaching Russian invasion of Königsberg, my father, who had been seriously wounded in Russia, was taken to the hospital in Hufen. At that time, it was naturally already too late for her to flee anywhere. Nonetheless, my father after having seen a lot of misery begged my mother to get out by all means, but that didn't help neither. We managed only once to visit my father in the hospital. He told us about the carnage and atrocities outside of Königsberg, and we were terribly afraid of what was in store for us all. From time to time, the Russians were driven back by the German soldiers from smaller localities. It was a constant coming and going, without an end. Then my father was somehow healed from his shoulder injury, but not quite. Then he was ordered again to fight on the front line, and that was ten days before the Russian invasion of the city. It hurt us all to lose our father again and nobody knew that it was forever. He never came back from Russia.

Our aunt Agnes came to us, virtually almost creeping close to the houses' walls to avoid the attack of the on-board weapons and said:

"I'm going with Karin over the Baltic Sea, as long as there's still a loophole somewhere, but our grandma, we can't take her with us. She's too sick and won't stand it anymore." We were all baff, because now my mother also had, besides us, to take care of Grandma. Well, they came then and brought the Grandma's belongings to us, and so we had another one we could lean on in our daily fear. People in the cellar became more nervous from day to day. All sat there with sinister faces, and no one knew what was in store for them in the coming days and nights. We only heard the sounds of Stalin's organs. We saw only burning houses from cellar holes. The door of our anti-aircraft shelter flew up and down because of mighty air pressure. The young soldiers, who were crouching in our cellar, trembled with fear and could not leave, because the command was: "Defence!" People always said to them, "Run away and try to get home."

And they did it after all. Where they went, who knows? Now everyone noticed again and again that something had to happen. The situation had got scary. There were rumors, the Russians were already close to the city, and we all also realized it.

The Russians are coming

On 9 April 1945, early in the morning, at five o'clock, it did happen. Through shots and strikes of grenades we didn't hear at all that burning shots flew over our house and everything above us was in flames. The upper part of the house didn't exist anymore, and the stairwell was burning. My mother and other people ran down the basement gangways hectically searching for the opportunity to get alive out of there. The thick smoke was already crawling through all the joints. Then, they all came back running; they were quite excited and shouted, "How can we get out now?"

Suddenly, strange-sounding cries reached our ears. Those were the voices of women and men in Russian. They had penetrated from the neighbouring cellar; its wall had been broken through. We couldn't get there from our room. They all came to our basement with planted bayonets, one after the other. Some Russian women were ahead of them. We got scared stiff. They stood before us pushing the people and shouting with rage the words, "Hwatche, Hwatche, Hwatche!" and again and again the same, but none of us knew what that was.

Suddenly, one Russian woman sprang out in front of my mother and yelled again the words, "Hwatche, Hwatche!" My mother then grabbed the alarm clock and wanted to give it to her; she thought they wanted to know what time it was, but that one started shouting at her in rage. She put the rifle on my mother. We clung to the mother scared to death, and the woman cut a few steps back. She didn't want to know the time, but a golden wristwatch. My aunt Helga, who had come to us with her son Harald a few days ago, told us: "Asta, give her the watch, or she'd blow you away." They got her watch and the watches of all other people as well and ran away. The next batch came just behind them and ransacked the whole cellar.

We already saw our end. The smoke was getting stronger and we were afraid not to be able to get out of the burning house. Suddenly, the last Russians turned around and drove us all out of the cellar. We slowly squeezed through the passage and were at heart jolly glad, not to be burned alive. The neighbouring staircase had been already surrounded by flames, but we managed. Now we stood in the hallway and saw the sea of flames on the road. Tanks were rushing into the city, and the people were driven by the Russians in the opposite direction.

Driven as cattle

Then suddenly, Russians stormed towards us. They cried from behind at us shouting out "Dawai, dawai, dawai!"; and many people also got the rifle butts on their backs as my aunt Helga who almost collapsed with pain. As we all got out of the house, they drove us up the street like cattle.

It was a chaos with so many people, almost only women, children and old people running confused. We had clung to our mother like monkeys and were dead scared, we could be torn apart. After we had covered about 200 meters, we noticed near the Oberhaberberg church that our old granny was suddenly not to be seen anymore. My mother got excited and wanted to turn back to look for her, but that wasn't possible, not at all. The Russians continued to drive us further on like cattle. There was no return for anyone. My mother went on crying for her mother, but in vain. She was gone. Then she shouted at my aunt Helga: "Watch the children too, or we'll also lose them!"

I with my brother Hans clung to Aunt Helga's hands and we kept moving on plagued with the thought, where our grandma might have gone away? We all were crying and we couldn't believe she wasn't with us anymore. We kept on shouting, "Grandma, Grandma, where are you?" But she was missing.

The trek of people passed the main railway station, then moved further across the rails of the goods train station. There were dead soldiers everywhere, Germans and Russians. That was a horrible look, they were terribly mutilated. Once I cried out in horror, because I saw a Russian tank rolling onto us. He then made a turn to the right, and there lay a wounded German soldier, and the tank then crushed him and this before our eyes. I saw also how the body was jerking. It was terrible, we all cried out of fear.

Suddenly my mother fell over the rails. She got a kick from a Russian soldier. It was a face I had never seen in my life before:

broad and slit-eyed. We all screamed. I had never seen such an ugly doing before. He pulled off the only piece of luggage out of my mother's hand and ran away with it. It was the suitcase with all our documents. Other people were also mishandled like that. That was the prey catching. Now we had only our naked lives to defend or to lose.

We were further driven towards Ponarth, a suburb. We had been already so broken with thirst and hunger, but we knew, there was nothing for us. And so we were driven further and further away. Suddenly I saw a blue scooter lying on the road. I grabbed it and put my little sister Eva on it and from now on pushed her. Because she was only four years old and couldn't keep up with us any longer. My brother Herbert and I always were pushing it in turns. We were trying to see to it that we were keeping together in that confusion. Until now, we had seen nothing but corpses; they lay around in all directions. And as we were out of Ponarth, we had to turn off to an unpaved road.

Then a forest came right and left, and we all had to stop. Everyone was brooding over what was going to happen now, and we were seized with a nagging fear. The Russians went into the crowd of people and caught women for them. All people screamed out of fear, "No, no, no!" But it didn't help. They hauled women and dragged them into the forest. They ripped their clothes off their bodies and pounced on them. For us children, the world collapsed with horror. We all had to look at how young and older women were bestially raped by the barbarians; the soldiers stood by the women one after another waiting for their turn. None of these women came back to the trek again; they had been partly ruined to death because of so much ordeal. That went on until the night; and the next day, in the morning, we even saw some raped women hanging on trees. Half-naked and bloody. It was disgusting for us to look at it. The Russians had done it as a deterrent for all of us and for the German soldiers. They would have also to see it, when they would be driven by. We children had pressed our hands in front of the eyes and only cried fearing it could happen to our mother the same way.

Into the unknown

Then, some kind of relief came down, as the Russians yelled at us ordering to get up, and then, sometime later, we continued our march further through the countryside. Everywhere on both sides of the road, women, children and soldiers were lying in and around the roadside ditches, sometimes killed, raped or just fallen exhausted. Who knows it? Stolen and torn items were also scattered all around, but none of us could even touch a piece of it. We had to keep on going and all of us had no strength at all to bear up for a long time.

The very first remained already lying on the road and no one took care of them; after the first distress the self-sustaining instinct drove everyone further. The ones, who stayed behind, got from Russian soldiers a farewell stroke with the rifle butt, and then it was the end for them. While we were again slowly trotting further for quite a while, a Russian came suddenly towards me and tore me the scooter out of my hands. My little sister fell and could hardly walk. Now my mother had to take my sister on the shoulders and carry her. But it didn't last long, the strength was soon away. My aunt Helga then replaced her, and so they were doing by turns.

We were weeping from exhaustion, thirst and hunger, but there wasn't anything anywhere for us. People were getting more and more distressed with every day and hour. The Russians noticed that. They worked out a plan for us. We came to a big place and saw a big farm standing in the background. There we saw only Russian soldiers ahead of us who dragged the stolen things of people back and forth. They shouted at each other like animals, and we couldn't understand a word. All at once, we spotted a well there, and everyone rushed there to drink something real for the first time. People virtually beat themselves for a bit of clear water. Aunt Helga had a water bottle and we filled it a couple of times to stuff ourselves with enough water. Then we were herded together and were not allowed to leave the place. People shouted that we all were hungry and that again and again. But no one gave us anything. It went to the evening, and people were very afraid of what might be in store for us.

After some time a lot of Russians came suddenly into the crowd; they were saying repeatedly: "Dawai, dawai, poschli!" and people dashed in confusion. They had to line up in rows, and then the Russians came up to us, started counting always pointing their fingers at the people: "Ras, dwa, dri, out! Ras, dwa, dri, get out!" That meant, every third person had to get out from the line and then it was always a woman. Women had to go the left, were there a man or a child, then it was said to the right. Then women were driven to a barn and men as well as children – to a stable.

A panic broke out among the people, but it was all in vain. They had to endure it. The women shouted for their children. They were again raped there in the cruellest way, and the men... they were just old grandpas. All watches and rings were taken off from them by the Russians, and they even had to open their mouths, the Russians wanted to see, if the men had dentures with gold teeth. The ones who had them had to hand off their dentures; it was bad for children to witness all that. Then the utterly maltreated women came one by one from the barn to the stable and looked for their children. Partly blood-smeared, half-naked and entirely emotionless, they plunked themselves down somewhere on the floor. So was also my aunt Helga. She was completely ruined and just only crying. Her son Harald and my mother tried to clean her body from the blood with straw, but it didn't come off. That was a shock for the 11-year-old Harald and for us to see something like that.

No one was allowed to leave the stable, there were sentinels with planted bayonets everywhere around and all of us were in sight.

We were terribly afraid of what would come next. In the evening, Russian women in uniforms and with guns came all of a sudden to us; they looked at everything what could suit them, and then went to the women who were still wearing fur coats. They requested them to take off their coats and went away with them. The women were now standing there in the cold without coats and were freezing terribly. Some people took off their sweaters and gave them to them. We were still guarded, and everyone was thinking about what they had to do with us. The rapes went on again during the night.

My mother and Aunt Helga were very much scared that they possibly had to go with them. We children crawled closely together and gathered so much straw that we hid my mother and Aunt Helga underneath. We even sat still on them and the Russians didn't notice the trick. We were lucky, they got safe away. Early in the morning we were all driven out into the yard and later – into the barn. There we all got some water to drink and a slice of Russian bread. It was as heavy as lead and tasted horrible, but hunger brought it into our stomachs. We had to stay there all day and were guarded all the time. The following night, the Russian soldiers pulled women out of the barn again, and everyone screamed in despair. The panic took hold of us, and we ran with my mother to a haystack and my aunt and her son behind us. We crawled as fast as we could into the pile and didn't dare to quit the hideout. We might have fallen asleep later because of the fatigue, and the next morning we were awakened only by the calls of the Russian soldiers.

As I crawled around in the hay, I bumped into a hard object thinking it might have been one of my siblings and cleared the object with my hands. I was so scared when I saw that it was a German soldier without his head. I got into a panic, and I shrieked out loud calling my mother. I trembled all over my body and had to vomit right off. The Russian soldiers came to us immediately and looked around at first. Then they pulled the soldier out of the hay and laid him in the middle of the barn. It had to be a deterrent for all of us. My mother and other siblings locked me very firmly in their arms, and so I gradually calmed myself down. Almost all people were crying in view of so much brutality, and the soldier remained lying there.

On the trek

We all were herded together and had to line up outside. There came a Russian truck then, and a few soldiers jumped down. We thought it was over, but it was different. Again they gave us a little water to drink and a slice of that lead bread, which tasted as if it had been baked in the car oil. But we choked it down. After hours many people felt so queer that they had to vomit just on the highway while dragging on with the trek. No doubt, it was because of that bread we had eaten. I guess we were right about the car oil. In the evening, we also felt really wretched and had to vomit. Many felt so bad that they weren't able to keep up with the rest of us. They were left in the ditches by the road, and no one took care of them. Each one was worrying about own life.

We spent the night at the edge of a forest; the soldiers guarded us from all sides. The women tried to hide under trees, but they were spotted everywhere, and many had to go up the trucks. They were then raped again and..... always the screams. My mother had a guardian angel until now; however they had already taken my aunt many times.

At dawn, we were again on the road and driven like cattle on it. People had already been so weakened that they were going slower and slower. That didn't suit the Russians, and they dealt out blows with their rifles right and left. Many people screamed in pain, but that didn't bother the Russians and they carried on beating them. My mother also got a blow to the low back and flew to the ground in pain. But the will to live is so strong, anyhow. She got herself up then and slogged along with us further on.

Suddenly, we saw people without an end coming to us from

the opposite direction. They all were German soldiers probably driven to a collection point. They were guarded and were not allowed to stop to talk with us. So we all went past each other without saying a word to anyone, otherwise they probably could have got blows. And those convoys with imprisoned soldiers were very big; we had to witness it later.

After we had marched several hours and the weariness began more and more to overcome all of us, the Russians must have worked out a plan for us. They stopped us all and, always pointing to the mouth in form of a sign language, made it clear to us that we all would get something to eat. But it turned out to be different. They drove us down from the road to some paths laid out with logs, and suddenly people noticed that this was a trap, because the ground beneath us was shaky. We found ourselves in moorland. Everyone got terribly scared and confused. Then we saw soon some people sinking in the swamp, they didn't come out again. It was horrible to look at how they called for help, and no one could help. We children were screaming "Mama, Mama, hold us firmly!" We firmly clung like monkeys to my mother trying not to slip away from the pathway laid out with wooden logs. Suddenly, my little sister Eva fell down slipping off the log. She suddenly stuck in the swamp too, and then one quick-witted woman behind Eva pulled her swiftly out. She was fully in mud, but we engulfed her in a hug and were happy to have her saved.

Having covered in that manner a few stretches without being able to look around, we saw a big barn at some distance, and everyone knew already what the Russians were going to do with us again. Many women still tried to flee, but it was useless. They didn't come far. The swamp had devoured them. That was the worst thing that we children had seen so far.The people were driven then into a big barn, and the Russian soldiers stood there again waiting already for us. They immediately picked out again the women and pushed them to the ground in the building standing behind the barn. We pushed our mother in the corner to the ground, and laid us on her. Now she was pretty much covered with our little bodies and hardly got any air to breathe, but she was enduring it, and we were afraid to get up. The soldiers pounced on women with their trousers pulled down. In view of such atrocities our childish hearts nearly jerked to a halt out of fear. One couldn't believe that a person could do something like this without even having any pangs of remorse. I wouldn't be able to recover from these horrible things for the rest of my life and I can't forget having seen something like that at the age of ten. My little soul had got thereby a big crack in life.

We stayed crouched on my mother all night long and didn't know where my aunt Helga with Harald stayed. We found out the next morning that our aunt Helga with Harald were not far away from us behind a pile of wood, and they had covered themselves with straw, and so she had great luck that night. Now all who could still go were driven out again. Partly half naked, and everything had been torn out on them. And so it went on again without food and drink. That's why many people couldn't get on any longer because of thirst and hunger. When we were on the highway, it began to rain, and we really caught the drops just to get something wet to the mouth. Later, people threw themselves to the ground to drink what was in the puddles. My little sister Eva also drank from it. A few days later she got dysentery and many other people too. None could treat it with drugs, and people became weaker and weaker.

My mother turned out to be inventive. As we were driven through a destroyed village, she started looking for a charred beam or wood.

At one burned down house she broke out of the trek and ran as fast as she could to such a beam, scratched out with her bare hands some black stuff from it and quickly came back to us, but no one did anything to her. She rubbed the mass to a powder and gave it to Eva to eat. She reluctantly took the stuff and that she did every day until it was used up. There was nothing she could be cured with. She became so weak that we all carried her alternately. We were joined by more and more people who came from somewhere.

A few days later, we arrived at a place where only some barracks stood. Mountains of grenades had been piled all around there. We all were driven to that place. The women and the old men had to stack the grenades on trucks. This went on up to the darkness, and here and there blows were given out to the people who couldn't do the job the way the soldiers wanted. We kids had to watch all this. We were crying out of fear that something might happen to our mothers. After that everyone had to go to the barracks for the night. But they were so dirty that no one dared to lie down on that bare ground. But the fatigue and weakness overwhelmed us.

In the morning, there was again a bit of water and a piece of that "oil bread". The people devoured it like animals. We hadn't received a warm meal during the whole time of our trek, only some water and bread. A few hours later we had to move again through fields and small deserted localities. We were never allowed to stop over there. Why? None of us knew that. In case we were brought to a halt, then only on the way or where barns and stables were.

Back to Königsberg

All this wandering took about five weeks, and then we all realized that it was going back to Königsberg, just the other way, from a different direction. Both young and old had lost all interest in life. After a long night on an open field we all, being constantly guarded by the Russians, were again herded up together early in the morning, so that no one would be able to run away somewhere. Then they counted how many women, children and old people were there. A lot of people had already perished owing to weakness, rape and hunger. We weren't even allowed to bury them. The people were putting up with it emotionless, because they did not know whether they themselves could be the next.

Now we saw already the first ruins of Königsberg, and a kind of hope arose in the people. But until then, no one knew what would be in store for us. We came back to Ponarth and were driven in the direction of the Schichau shipyards. Then we found ourselves in Unterhaberberg district and saw dead bloated horses lying on a long road. Just as many decaying human bodies were lying around. It was a hell for all of us to come upon something like that. All the houses were in ruins, we saw only mountains of garbage, junk, and still burning houses. It was hard for us to get through. We felt that we were driven to the city center.

Suddenly we all had to stop, because it was already getting dark, and we were divided into groups, each of about 30 people. Our group, which also included the son of our aunt Helga, was now driven in a house that remained intact to some extent. We had to divide up; 15 people went into the right room and the rest into the opposite one. Nobody knew why. Late in the evening, we got again a bit of water to drink. It had been dragged in by the Russians in large zinc buckets, and each of us also had got a half of that oil bread. It tasted terrible, but it was eaten like cakes, we all were so terribly starved out.

No one was allowed to leave the building. We all had to do the necessities in the backyard. It was terrible to be watched there too. Later, as some people had already thrown themselves on the ground to get a wink of sleep, it was impossible to drop off, because we heard a cry from the outside. Those were the Russians who came to us. They were shining around with flashlights in their hands. We all got blinded, and they ordered us to get up. Then they again started looking for women, as always, when it got dark. They took who they wanted. Our aunt Helga was there again, too. All women were pushed back into the hallway. There was a room where they all had to get in. Outdoors, on the way during the trek, it was terrible for us children to take it in, but here in the rooms it was even more terrible. My cousin Harald sat there and only held his hands on his ears because his mother was also there. As hours later the aunt came back to us, she looked dead and only stared ahead frozen in shock and didn't say anything at all. After a little while, she was packed with crying fits and her whole body was terribly trembling. We couldn't help her.

Outlawed

The Russians had disgraced everything. We found out that our guards, who had been defiling us for weeks, were suddenly gone and we were free as birds at once. From now on, everyone went his own way without having the other in the neck. The corpses of Russians were lying around in the streets and ruins, as well as of our soldiers and civilians. We just climbed over the dead. It was terrible. We had only one goal, and that was to get something edible for us. Now we rummaged in every halfway safe corner trying to find at least something. But thousands of people did the same. Everyone wanted to eat and to drink.

Our mother was besieged with the thought to find her own mother again. With pain and misery, we browsed through the streets, littered with corpses. It was stinking abominably. The debris made it very difficult for us to move along. And of course, the Russian military was omnipresent. It took us a few days to reach our previous apartment, and we all thought that our grandma might have reached the anti-aircraft shelter in the house where we lived. But as we got there, nobody was in the basement yet. Our house was completely burned-out and ruined; it looked like all other houses. The disappointment was great for my mother. The basement was littered with bed feathers. The Russians had slashed open all the remaining beds. Then we left our home in bewilderment and didn't know where to go to. Then we had to look for a new dwelling, but everywhere we looked, there were only ruins and mountains of garbage. We saw parts of dead bodies sticking out of the debris and thought that our grandma could lie under it. Such were our terrible thoughts.

At length, we found something where we could put up for the night. Those were two partly intact rooms on the lower floor of the house with former four apartments; all of them were in ruinous condition and totally smashed up by the Russians. The house was in Horst-Wessel-Straße close to the main railway station. The following night our mother and we all children took at first our ease on the bare floor, and we were glad to be able to sleep at least so.

Now we went out during the day searching for some useful things, but there was utter chaos in basements and ruins where we thought we could find something. We found a few jars of boiled fruit and rejoiced like kings, hefted them to our mother and had something to eat. The Russians were also searching everywhere for something edible. The soldiers themselves didn't have proper rations. They had only the millet gruel from a field kitchen every day. They didn't have any spare for us. They were rationed out piecewise with raw potatoes that they cooked on street bonfires made of stones and wood, just at the place where they used to be at the moment. We children besieged the area and were standing there like starving vultures. We were behind every fireplace hoping to get sometime a potato. Often we got one or several stones thrown at us, possibly out of anger that they might have been deeply embarrassed on their part not being able to give us at least something, because they themselves had nothing. And that was happening every day. Each of us siblings went their own way in the morning and never together. Everyone thought only of himself. This was immediately taken over by all children in the whole city.

So we turned into street children who only begged or looked out for something edible. We had also to take care of ourselves, not be ambushed and robbed by other older people. The two rooms that we now called our own had been barely furnished with two beds, which we had found in a cellar. We weren't accustomed to feather beds anymore. We had only our own clothes on and were unable to sleep properly, because the Russians could come into and go out of the Germans' scanty dwellings every time they wanted at night. There were only old people, children and women, and as all the doors had to remain open, according to Stalin's command; the Russian soldiers could get out women, girls, and even old grannies the way they wanted and then rape them. They did it just on the spot. There was no consideration for children. They had to witness everything.

Where is Grandma?

My mother had nothing in her head now but to look for our grandma. We went every day trying to find her when we weren't just on a begging tour. At first, we searched all over the streets, where we used to live before the Russians drove us out, and every pile of rubble. Where some parts of corpses were protruding, we digged around with bare hands in the hope of finding her underneath, but it was always in vain.

About four weeks later, when we were once more at work with a spade and a rake that we had found, we met by chance our aunt Helga with Harald; they were happy to have found us again this way. From then on, we lived together again in our two almost broken rooms, because they had not found a proper place to live yet. Now, as we believed, we had a little more protection around us again, because our cousin was one year older than me, and I moved along with him begging during the day.

Then my aunt said to my mother, "Asta! Let's try to go one day to Grandma's former garden in the Kontiner Weg. Maybe Grandma went there the night we lost her." Mother thought that it was impossible. Because of her bad legs and the mess the Russians made those days. But we decided to have a try and set off. It took us hours to get through the devastated streets, and when we got there, we found that the Russians were everywhere in the entire garden. They had stationed tanks and other equipment there, and they didn't want to let us get to the place, where the seemingly unhurt summerhouse of our grandma stood.

Aunt Helga, who spoke a little bit of broken Russian, asked if we could come in to look out for our grandma. They agreed, and we all were very excited. Now our mother and aunt went into the summerhouse and were appalled to find out that my mother's mother lay half-naked, raped and already halfway decayed in the middle of her refuge. They screamed stupefied with horror. We children went to them and couldn't believe that this could be our grandma. It was so terrible for us children. Mother begged one Russian for the permission to come once more with Aunt Helga to bury Grandma in her garden. He said, "Yes," and we went away in deep mourning.

The next day we all went back, and to our astonishment the Grandma wasn't in the summerhouse anymore. Aunt Helga went to one Russian and asked him, but he just chased us away, and thus our grandma was gone. My mother and we searched round about the whole borough, but it was in vain. We all were deeply distressed and our mother got sick because of that.

Survival

A terrible time began for all of us. Every day became an act of survival for each of us. There were new tasks to master every day. The more we lived on the streets, the harder we became against each other. That was just so. We ran and walked over the corpses, and it didn't bother us anymore. Everyone wanted and was only looking for something edible.

In my search I came to the former Bismarckstraße. It was full of charred corpses. The firebombs had probably caught the marching soldiers. I moved horror-stricken on and found a still intact handcart beside a house wall. I was happy like a queen, and thought about that we didn't need any more to drag the charred beams out of the ruins to make a fire at home. I immediately loaded the cart with some logs and beams scattered around. Then I drove it happily to my mother, and they all beamed with joy when I arrived with it.

I went off again with it the next day. I searched through one basement where I thought I could find something, then came to the backyard where there was a lot of stuff scattered around. Then I saw a half-open door leading to a storage room. I saw a big wooden box standing there. As I just wanted to step in to tear off the planks, I saw two feet protruding from underneath. At first I was totally paralysed by fear, then I looked in the box, and there was a dead, raped young woman in it. I pulled myself together, took the box apart and brought some slats to the cart. The feet had already been nibbled at by rats that were flipping around in all corners. My stomach got in a very queasy condition, but I thought: she wouldn't harm me anymore.

Weeks were passing by, and our situation was getting worse and worse. The whole city was just a pile of rubble. Nothing had been properly cleaned up anywhere. There were corpses lying everywhere and the stink in summer was abominable. The Russians started digging up the mass graves at the Castle Pond. The Russians brought trucks with limestone and some old German men had to pour it over the corpses so that the plague didn't break out. We often stood there watching it when we were begging just in the area.

And the cleanliness of the people had also been over. We didn't have any kind of laundry detergent, soap, etc. There wasn't even enough water, because everything lay in rubble and ashes. There was only one place in the city, where we could get a bucket of water for a day. It was a former police building in the district of Oberhaberberg, where people were standing in line every day hoping to get something. We all got the cockroaches' itches and lice. We had terrible itches; the lice under the scab fouled the skin, and no one helped us with drugs or the like. Our mother cut all hair from our heads to get the situation under control, but it was all for nothing. Neither got we rid of the lice nor of the scabies. It was terrible for us. We scratched ourselves sore.

One day, all Germans were brought together to the Russian commandant's office, and we had to line up. Then Russian nurses smeared up our bodies with the stuff they took from their buckets, and it looked like jam, so red was this grease. It burned like fire on the body. We had to go there again fourteen days later, but it didn't help at all. My brother Herbert had such bad scabies that when he pulled off his sole nightgown in the morning, it was all scabbed over. My mother always cried when she saw him standing so in front of her. She always had to take off his nightgown very cautiously; he always suffered from pain so terribly. It took an eternity till he got better again, and we all had to deal with it. There was no whining and no help from anywhere.

A few weeks later, many people in the city got typhus and died away like flies. An epidemic broke out. I also caught it, and the hair on my head fell out; it had just started growing on my baldness that had been cut by mother the way she had scissored hair of other family members. I was so sick that I could barely stand on my feet. My siblings always brought me something from their begging and searching bouts, but I couldn't eat anything. I constantly got from my mother crushed charcoal with some water and swallowed it down, but I had no willingness to go on living. Nevertheless, anyhow I was getting a little better bit by bit, and I picked myself up. And I went off on begging tours again.

Begging Tours

Our goal now was the railway yard; the Russian trains arrived there and then returned to Russia. When they arrived there for some hours to be cleaned up, we rushed in like lions searching everywhere, but always in vain. There happened to be here and there someone who gave us something: a chunk of bread or a few potatoes sometimes, but that was a matter of luck. Mostly we went to the camping places of Russian soldiers hoping to get something. We ransacked all the clutter that they had left looking for potato peelings and the like. We just looked like rats scrambling around in search of something edible.

One day, I found a whole fish in the pile of garbage. I ran overjoyed to my mother. "Girl, it's bad, it can't be eaten anymore." But I insisted on cooking it. There was nothing but water to spice it up, and mother flayed it. It just fell apart after that. We children ate it anyway to appease our hunger.

Sometimes, we went with our mother to the dock of the Schichau shipyard; there were still abandoned barges there, and we tried to get on them, but that was hardly possible, because Russians always guarded the barges, which were mostly loaded up with some goods: cereals, salt, coal, and other things. They unloaded all of them and divided the goods among themselves. We only managed sometimes to pick up several grains that had been shed. This went on for hours. Once they left a sack, and my mother said to us that we all had to get something out of there and we did it so. We were then closely watched by the Russians and were punished, because we had stolen; everything was taken away from us again, and our mother was then raped in an old shed nearby. We went back in despair, and since that our mother didn't take part in our bouts anymore. But my cousin Harald and I didn't let us get discouraged; a few days later we went back there, and we were lucky. My cousin said, "Ulla, you keep watch, and I'll fetch a full bag of grain." There was a guard post in one corner, but we were as quick as a wink and he didn't notice us. When it worked out, we ran home as soon as we could, and our mothers hugged us with joy. The grain was dried on the stove plate, and then we ground it in coffee mills by hand. Mother cooked a flour soup from this, without salt, etc., only with water. It was a Sunday dinner for all of us. We also made coffee from it. That was also prepared on our stove plate. The grains were thoroughly roasted and ground. So we eked out our living, day by day.

The situation was getting worse and worse in autumn and

winter. There was almost nothing left, and thousands of people starved to death in Königsberg. It was also hardly possible to find some wood to burn. There was no electricity in the whole city. In the evening we sat together only at open stove doors. It was also bad with clothes' washing. My mother and Aunt Helga always went to Horst Wessel Park. There was a pond in it, and there they built a makeshift jetty where they stood and rinsed off their clothes. We children always went with them as watchdogs, because Russians could rape women.

One day, it was a lovely Sunday with bright sunshine, and my mother was alone on the jetty. All of a sudden she saw a shadow behind her. She turned as quick as a wink round and pushed the Russian standing there off the jetty. He fell into the water and went down at first. We ran very fast away and saw from the wall that he was fighting for his life, because he couldn't swim. But we ran as fast as we could to our dwelling.

The Russians were always looking everywhere for some more or less intact rooms. They took up quarters directly opposite to ours, and we thought that we wouldn't have peace anymore because of them. We were very much scared, but we had to realize that there were also families with children there. Children are curious, and so we got together and started learning the Russian language. Some of them had also knives with them and stood then haughtily in front of us, beggar children, threatening us. We ran then as fast as we could to our mother. It caused a lot of trouble.

So we couldn't stay there any longer and had to look for another place to live in. We left the same day with the handcart and a few belongings in the direction of Unterhaberberg. My paternal grandparents with their siblings used to live there. We hoped to find one of them alive in that neighbourhood. We found a halfway undestroyed house in a backyard. But there were already some strangers living there. There was also a semi-inhabited house opposite to it. All of them were four stories high. There was a narrow courtyard lying in-between with a passage to the street.

Everything seemed somewhat ghostly tiny to us all. We children were all very much scared in there. It used to be our everyday routine to undertake the begging tours in the morning and as always, everyone for himself. Mother had started making friends with a woman nearly of her age who had a 14-year-old daughter; we found that she always had black clothes on and never went out alone. Only with her mother, if that. We learned then that she did it to protect her daughter from rape, but yet she had been ravished on many occasions. After some time, she probably got pregnant.

Now it was getting colder outside, and we thought if we would now search in areas around Königsberg, we'll might be able to find something edible there in the already harvested fields. We set out with good faith, but were bitterly disappointed, because there were already hundreds ahead of us who also believed they would find something there. The fields had been completely swept across. So the fight for the last survival got to be the order of the day. One day, my brother Hans went out in the morning and didn't come back to us in the evening. And we couldn't do anything because we didn't know in which direction of the city he had gone, and so we waited for him all night long in the dark room. Towards morning we heard heavy footsteps and a pitiful whimper. We understood right from the voice that it was our brother. Our mother ran to him and she saw that he had his whole knee broken and bleeding. His face was also blood-stained. He had been begging at the railway yard, and Russian soldiers had beaten him up there. As Hans became conscious again, he stumbled over the rails and made his way to us with terrible pain in his knees and face. The little guy not even nine-year-old was very brave for his age.

I had also befriended a Russian woman a few streets away. She was a high-ranking soldier. She had a small apartment with other soldiers there. It was in Steindamm-borough. Since there was only one waterhole at the police station, I also brought two buckets of water for her every other day. It took me over half an hour to get there walking. Hence, my command of Russian was also getting better and better. I spoke quite well already, and we had to assert ourselves everywhere to get over the hardships of everyday life. At some point, I came again to this woman and saw her uniform lying on the bed, and nearly a half of a rouble banknote was peeking out of her upper jacket pocket. I thought that I had to have it – no matter how – to buy a piece of bread on the black market for all of us. She was in the other room, and I seized the opportunity, took the note, then went into her room and asked if I should get some more water. She said yes, I picked up the buckets and stroke joyfully out. I first went to my mother, gave her the money and got the water. On returning, I handed over the water, the Russian woman gave me as usual a piece of bread, and I ran home. That's just misery, and it stops at nothing.

The story with the dog

Then a man moved into the room that was above us. He was a cobbler and occasionally soled shoes for Russian soldiers. One day, two Russians came to him, they had tied a dog down at the broken picket fence. My cousin and I saw it, and then Harald said, "Ulla, let's get the dog and slaughter it." – "You're crazy!" I said. "We need something to eat!" came back the answer. "It has to be fast. Let's go! We'll do it in!" And then the action kicked off. It was a black and white mongrel. Harald was the culprit; he took the dog to the non-functioning toilet and hit with an axe the front of its head. It screamed out, and Harald got panicked, he stuffed the dog in a bag, and ran quickly down to the basement. We padded through the cellar passageways of the adjacent building, and then he struck the dog dead. I was very queasy, but the thought that we would get something edible by doing so drove everything else out of my head.

We went back with the dog in the bag. Harald said, "Now we have to skin it, but we'll do it in our rooms." My mother had got seriously ill for a couple of days, she lay in the only bed that we had to share in our habitation and could not get up. Coming back we put at first the animal with the bag in a zinc tub and hid the tub under the mother's bed. She said, "That's out of the question. The tub must be taken away. If anyone finds it, it's all over for us." We begged, "Mum, let it stay there. Nobody would see it."

Suddenly, the man from above came in and two soldiers with him. One was a Mongol and looked terrible. The whole of his face was covered with smallpox scars. He looked just appalling. They said immediately to us, "Where's the dog that's in here?" We said we didn't have a dog and didn't see any. Of course, they didn't believe that and set out to search. As they stood by our mother's bed, this Mongol bent down and pulled out the zinc tub. A cursing storm in Russian burst out of his mouth; he immediately pulled out a pistol from his belt pointing it at my mother, and we all screamed terribly repeating, "No, no, no!" He stopped threatening with his pistol, and the other Russian said that if we don't get a new dog within seven days, he would come back and then something would happen. Our hearts got scared stiff. The Mongol asked again who killed the dog. Harald raised his finger. He took him outside and beat Harald so brutally up that he couldn't walk for days. We only cried, and were so much distressed because of all that. My mother said, "Do whatever you want with it. I wouldn't touch any piece of it even if I'll die." We plucked up all our courage. Harald couldn't do much anymore, but we still managed to pull the dog's skin off and cut it into pieces. Then the pieces were cooked in water, and we the kids ate that. We tasted it like a holiday roast.

Exactly one day later we set off looking for a new dog; my brothers and I just went to a barracks camp of the Russians. There, dogs were running around, and we were very lucky that a cute brown dog ran into us. We caught it at once and ran with joy to our mother, because she had already got discouraged disbelieving that we could manage to find one dog again. Unfortunately, we didn't have anything to feed the dog with, and it had to go hungry with us. It got only water. The next day the two Russians came back to us and wanted to see, if we had a new dog. They were very happy to have one again. The dog went right away with them without murmuring; and one Russian said to our mother that he wanted to bring us some wheat. The next day he came back and brought us about five pounds of wheat. We were all overjoyed.

Hunger winter 1946

The winter of 1946 was a disaster for all of us. There was a terrible cold that didn't want to end. Just as many people froze to death as they died of hunger. It was a chaos. Now there were more dead people lying around on the streets. Burial teams didn't manage at all to get people away. Mass graves were being dug out again everywhere. We barely dared to get out because of such bitter cold, but hunger drove us to do it.

Every day we went to the railway yard to beg. Like rats, we searched all the tracks and corners in the hope of finding something edible that the Russian women might had swept out of their trains, but mostly everything was in vain. We used to rob each other or sometimes even beat for a piece of bread, which the soldiers gave us sometimes, or we were allowed to scrape out the field kitchen if there was still some millet pudding (kasha) left, or it could happen that one or the other Russian couldn't eat his food. Then children got it in their cookware. We were always carrying beggar's bags around, which we called Prada-bags.

One day, I was also walking along the rails and picked up a chunk lying on the ground, thinking I found a piece of bread that had got frozen. On coming home I first let the chunk thaw out. A bit later, I wanted to see, whether it had thawed enough, and I was horrified to discover that what I had considered to be a piece of bread had been a pile of human excrement. My mother was so sad about it that she hugged me, what hadn't happened for a long time. She comforted me for a while, but I simply couldn't get over the thing I had brought.

One day, our mother said to us, we should go again to our old apartment and see if the house in the suburban Langgasse was still standing, or if the Russians had already knocked down the ruin. All the houses were burnt out, and those that were relatively intact had been intentionally set on fire. Everything was burning. The whole city stank of fire forever and ever. So we moved there, and as we stood there watching everything, my mother said, "I'd like to see if we still can get into our air-raid shelter." It all looked so strange, as if there was someone in there. The cellar shafts were a bit open, and my mother said that my brothers Herbert and Hans should stay outside and take care that no Russian came down to the cellar.

Then my mother and I decided to go there. My mother threw herself against the door of air-raid shelter, but it didn't work out. Then we tried together and the door opened. Right off, we were overwhelmed by an abominable stench. In the middle of the room, there was a lifeless body laid out on a stack of some other corpses; a small hatchet with a swastika pennant was stuck in the body. The Russians had beaten a German soldier to death; and they left him lying there as a deterrent to others. He had fully decayed already; and we quickly searched the cellar with our hands over our mouths trying to find something useful. Then we went outside very quickly.

Only away from here

In any case, the condition of the people still remaining in our city was getting worse and worse. Every day, while I was on my way begging, I was thinking about the coming day when I would have to die. I got more and more scared.

One day, I left our dwelling again alone, and was very much sad at heart. Walking around, I was only weeping and suddenly saw myself standing in the railway yard. I had hardly noticed what places I had been walking about. I knew from stories that many children had left from here with the only train leaving for Russia. Hours went by, and then I noticed a freight train being loaded by the Russians. I thought there might be a corner somewhere where I could hide myself away, and then I would just go with it. I walked along the train from both sides, up and down. Then, that might have noticed one Russian who asked me in Russian, if I wanted to go with. I said "Yes" and thought, "Gosh! I'm lucky to get out of here." I didn't think about anyone anymore and only felt the urge to save my own life.

The soldier picked me up and put me behind a large box in a hiding place, and said quietly in Russian, I had to be quiet, so that none of other Russians saw and heard me. They all sat around a potbelly stove and were playing cards. I got suddenly very scared and my whole body started shivering. The Russian noticed it and gave me a wadded military coat. I put that on the floor and snuggled into it. It took a good while, and then the wagon door was pushed shutting it up. Suddenly the train got jerking under way. I was so scared and pressed my face into the coat so that no one could hear me crying. Suddenly my siblings and mother crossed my mind, but there was no turning back for me now. The worst thing was that I didn't really know where I was going to. The train drove all night at a snail's pace, and I didn't dare to move being in sheer fear. I really did have a great guardian angel with me.

After a long drive, the train stopped; now I don't know what I was thinking of at that moment. I simply just couldn't think about anything. The Russian pulled me out from behind the box, pushed the gate open and heaved me into a deserted station. I only saw the rails under me. He shouted in Russian, I should run away very fast. I followed his words and ran along the train.

Suddenly, the train went on again, and I stood there all alone, overcome by fear and panic. I didn't even dare to take a step.

I saw then that some men were approaching me and started running over the rails. I came to a building, ran around it and then stood on a street. It must have been very early, because I could hardly see any people walking down the street. I hoofed it being hungry and thirsty, and then a woman wearing a headscarf came over to me. She spoke Russian to me, asked me what I was doing so late in the street. So I told her my name and where I came from. She told me that I am here in the country of Lithuania and the city is called Kowno (Kaunas). But I didn't know where and what that was. She took me with her. She lived with five or six children in a small hut; its floor was laid out with straw. The children lay on it and slept. She told me that I should also go there and lie down to have a bit of sleep. Surely, she noticed how tired I was. After sleeping, I think it was about noon, I got something to eat from her, and she treated me very well, just like her own children. Then I left her.

I noticed that I was in a completely different city and people were different too. Towards evening, that huge fear came over me again and I experienced terrible hunger and thirst. I passed a bakery – I had already forgotten what that actually meant – rushed in and begged for a piece of bread. The people might have realized immediately that I was a German beggar-child. I learned later that we, German children, were also called wolf kids by Lithuanians. I ate a half-fresh bread like a greedy wolf, so starved I was. We had forgotten what bread was and I couldn't imagine the taste of it anymore.

As I sat there on the steps in front of the bakery, a man came in and started looking at me through the shop window; then he opened the door and spoke to me in German. I thought why he could German? Was he perhaps also a German? But he was a teacher, as I learned a bit later, and wanted to take me home. I talked to him then. He asked me where my parents were and if I still had siblings. I don't know what was wrong with me, but I said I had no parents and no siblings anymore. I got afraid that he would send me back.

"Have they all already died?" he asked. I said, „Yes". He talked to the baker in a language I didn't understand, then turned back to me and asked, if I would like to join his family. That wouldn't be so far away from the city. I had never in my life travelled in a passenger car and could experience it for the first time. We drove for quite a while, and I didn't care. Suddenly we stopped. It was a hilly area. The man's cottage was so nice situated on the hillside, and we had to go up a long, snow-covered stair. When the door opened, I saw a well-dressed woman and two girls older than me. They looked quite startled, as if asking who really their father has dragged along with him. He waved me into a beautiful room, and I had to sit down. Then they conferred for some time about me. The man called me by my name and said that they wanted to keep me until I was well again getting rid of cockroaches' itches and the lice.

I was the happiest human being. Nobody would believe what was happening in my soul. I didn't ever want to go back. They bathed me in a large zinc tub and a couple of times, one after another. Then I got a long nightgown, and my things were burned, most probably because of the clothes' lice. Then we ate together, and all I know is that I had spent a lot of hours in a beautiful white bed until I finally opened my eyes. I felt in that family like being in a fairyland and didn't want to think about anything that would rupture wounds. I just blossomed there, but the man kept asking me about my parents, and at some point, I said that my mother with my siblings lived in Königsberg. From then on, the man repeatedly told me, I had to go back to my mother. She might have been very much worried about me, I should understand that. They also wanted to give me a lot of food for everyone and a backpack so that I could carry everything. I recovered well during the four weeks, got a little bit stronger again, and once more had the pluck to go back.

Home

And it did happen one day. The people packed everything for my mother and my siblings. I went back to the Kaunas railway station with the teacher. The man had driven me there; he knew exactly when the trains were leaving. It was so towards evening, and he talked to some Russian soldiers. They came up to me, lifted me with the valuable backpack in the compartment, and sometime later it went in the direction of Königsberg. The train jogged across the country for a long time, and I suddenly felt a huge fear that I might not be able to find my mother and siblings or that they might have already starved to death. I was only weeping, because I didn't know what would happen to me. A few Russian soldiers noticed that, and they asked me where I was going to. I said, "To my mother in Konigsberg." Then they left me alone. I only had my backpack in mind, which was packed full with bacon, bread, flour, sugar and salt. I myself wore a coat, sweater, skirt, underwear, shoes and self-made stockings. I had received this all from these very nice people. Now I was afraid of being attacked by begging children in Königsberg.

The journey was soon over, and it was already morning light when we arrived back at the railway yard of Königsberg. I asked a Russian soldier, if he could help me to get away from the station, so that no one would steal my backpack there. He was a bit older and also carried my backpack, because he surely couldn't watch how I struggled with trying to carry it. I was only a scraggy human being. Then he took me safely out of the beggars' area, and I headed to the half-burned-out dwelling, where we used to live before my departure. I kept on thinking, I would hopefully find them, and at that moment I was also somehow very proud of myself that I had performed a good deed being able to bring them something to eat. I felt like having a lump of gold with me.

I got to the dwelling, where they were actually still living and was very happy, but then I had to experience something between joy and fear because they were all very ill and could hardly move being undernourished and hungry. I became just as sad as before, as I saw that misery. My mother didn't know what to say, when she saw me again after nearly four weeks away. She just said, "Ulla, where have you been? We all thought you might have died."- "But, Mummy," I said sadly, "I've been to Lithuania and brought some very good things for you."

My siblings didn't respond at all to me reappearing there again. They pounced like wolves on all the things. Only my mother, she didn't care at all about what was happening. She wasn't even able to see the situation. I couldn't understand it and constantly appealed to her, "Mum, now eat something!" But she didn't really want to. She just kept on saying, we all would have to die soon, but I didn't want that anymore, got terribly scared, and told her that I was going back to Kaunas to see the family where I was. They saved my life, and I wanted to go back there. I begged, "Mum, let's all go there! I know now, how we all can get there." But she refused everything. Then I got angry and said, "Then I'll go alone there again!"

I was like obsessed with saving my life and always said to Mum that I didn't want to die like the others. She might have felt sorry for that too, and later said to me, "Would you find the way there again?" – "Yes Mum, I know exactly, how we'll get there." She was very, very weak and could barely walk properly. My siblings were lying being gravely ill. There was another woman in the next room, she had lost her only daughter because of rape; so my mother contacted her and asked, whether she would take care of the kids for a short while, if she would go to Lithuania for a couple of days. I had brought food now, and that would be enough for everyone, including her, for days. The woman said, "Mrs Wedigkeit, you gave your help to my daughter at the time, now I'll do it for your children."

With mother from Königsberg to Kaunas

We started that very evening, and I did the same at the railway yard as I did the first time. I approached a soldier who peeked out from a small window in the freight train and asked, if he would hide us in the waggon as far as Kaunas. We wanted to get something to eat for our sick siblings. We were lucky. He made a hand signal, looked around first, and then we crawled in on all fours into the waggon, squatted in a corner, and waited. Then I said to my mother, "Mum, why didn't you take Herbert, Hans and Eva with you?" – "Ulla, that wouldn't have worked out. They're way too weak to hold out. If we're back in a few days and they're a bit stronger, then we all go away. They are well looked after by Mrs. Neumann with what you have brought."

I thought about it and suddenly began to cry terribly, so that the Russian said, if I didn't stop, we had then to get out again. I got scared and behaved then quietly not to be kicked out. My mother was staring listless into space and didn't utter a word.

Then finally the train began to move, and three more Russians jumped into the waggon, closed the gate for the journey, and we had to hold out being hidden in the corner behind some machine parts. The Russian who had let us in told us in the beginning that he would throw us out when we stop in Kaunas. We didn't dare to utter a word believing that someone from the three could hear us. It was awful for us to squat like that. The cold crawled all over our bodies, and that rattle of the train rocked our marrows and legs. It was so, as if there was no end to it. I got a panic fear and thought to myself alone, "Hopefully the train will also stop in Kaunas." As the hours went by, and the sky grew brighter, I quietly said to my mother that we would soon come to Kaunas. She was very quiet and said nothing. Then I got even more afraid and thought, maybe she would not manage to get out of the train at all. I began to weep terribly again. My mother took then my face and pulled it slowly in her lap, so that the Russians wouldn't notice me crying.

At some point, the train stopped and the Russians pushed open the gate. They all got out, and that one came back again to us. "Matka poschli, poschli, dawai!" Mother and I could barely get up from stiffness and coldness in our bones. We trembled all over and crawled like animals out of the waggon. We thanked him and got the impression that he was overjoyed to get rid of us. We staggered very wobbly over the railway tracks and had to walk for a while until we reached the station. But we had managed to get to Kaunas.

My mother was soy weak; she needed to eat something at first. I left immediately and begged off a few shops outside the station for something to eat and got something. Overjoyed I went to my mother who had sat down on a bench in the station building to warm up herself a bit. At least, there was a heated place somewhere. The cold was everywhere in February. We sat definitely a few hours there to get well again and to find out, where we were after all. But then we pulled ourselves together and went through the streets of Kaunas. It appeared so alien to us and we got afraid to be caught up, because the Russians were also everywhere and they controlled the whole city.

We decided not to stay long and first searched for the area where I had spent the last few weeks. It took us quite a while to find it. Kaunas isn't so small, and I had to search for a long time. We also managed to put up for the night here and there, but we learned later that it was forbidden to keep Germans.

In the daytime we were begging. It was a difficult time because mother wasn't feeling well. We met very different people. Some welcomed us kindly; others despised or even spat at us and cursed us, "You Nazi pigs! Get out of here!" I was a child at the age of ten, and I had no idea about Nazis. It all hurt so much and I only had sad thoughts. I always asked my mother why people were so angry with us. After all, we didn't do anything. I think two or three weeks had passed away till I rediscovered the area where I had found a shelter. As I showed up with my mother, they didn't know whatsoever what to do, they got so much scared. They took me very firmly in their arms and were happy that I was back. They first provided my mother with something better than the things she had on her body. We had only rags with lice. People kept us for a few days and I didn't want to leave. We felt well there. But my mother wanted to go back to Königsberg and take her children.

Out into the country

We also got some food from the people, and the man drove us to Kaunas railway station. Now we had to realize that there were many Russians who controlled everything they were suspicious of. It wasn't possible to get away from there, and some Russians already started eyeing us, as if trying to find out, what we were looking for there. We noticed that and got somewhat scared that they would surely arrest us soon. Mother said we had to get out of there; otherwise they would lock or deport us, in the long run. The man had possibly also seen that there were so many Russians there and was quickly gone. So we left the station and went to Kaunas to beg again.

As we walked through the streets, we noticed that there were quite a few cliques of German children begging off something to eat. But we were only thinking of the children at home. How do we get to Königsberg? Everything was blocked. It was terrible for us. We had to be very careful not to be caught up by the Russians. They were everywhere now, and the whole country was occupied by the Russians. We begged civilians in their houses and we also tried in some shops, but it was more difficult, because there were always Russians coming in and going out there. We went back to the train station and wanted to get away, but it didn't work out. My mother became more and more silent and hardly said a word.

Now we made up our minds to get quickly out of the city. But it turned out quite differently. There was a big snowmelt in the spring, and the whole city was under water. Besides, we also had to beg people for shelter to have a place to stay. It was awfully cold and wet everywhere; we didn't have any due clothing to have on in such cold weather. Before the water rose in the city, we slept in open doorways to have a roof over our heads. We were very fortunate that while begging we met a family who put us up. They had four children, and the father made blue-dyed headscarves and linen according to patterns of ancient Lithuanian traditions. We could stay for about three weeks there. They also fed us, for which we were so much thankful to them.

My mother had only one thought, how we could get to Königsberg. We went to the station again when the flood was over, but again the Russians were there and kept everything under control. When the water was gone, we wanted to get out into the country. There, we thought, there wouldn't be so many Russians.

We footed it to the little wooden houses to beg for something. They all were too far apart from each other. We didn't feel so much pursued anymore and somehow freer. Every day we walked from ten to thirty kilometres through the country and always along either bank of the Memel to have the orientation. Thus, we were somewhere else every day and no longer met so many children from Königsberg or elsewhere who begged just as we did. I thought only of my siblings and asked my mother again and again when we would go back, "Mother, when are we going to go back? Mother, they need food." My mother got so strange and didn't answer my questions anymore. She was only staring dead ahead. I was very sad about it and really suffered from the state of things. We were going further and further into the interior of the country, and it turned us into real highway beggars.

Watch out!

We had to be very much careful not to be caught by Russian soldiers. They drove through Lithuania day and night. But also here, people were not allowed to host begging children and women. This was punished with the deportation to Siberia. People were very scared and avoided us, wherever they could. But some still took us for a night, be it a stable or their barn, sometimes a tiny apartment.

Most of the time, we slept out of doors in the woods or in the fields; in summer, under haystacks and straw dolls that had been set up on grain fields. At daytime, we went only over the countryside and through forests. Guerrilla warfare between the Russians and the Lithuanians was going on in the whole country during that time. It was terrible what we often saw, when Russians went to small Lithuanian villages at night and killed off whole families that didn't fit into the Russians' way of thinking. Often it was a betrayal instigated by differently minded neighbours. The Lithuanian partisans wore the edelweiss sign on their caps and the Russians – a red star.

One night, we stayed with a family who put straw on the floor for us. It was just a clay floor, as it was in all the houses made of timber beams. We were glad to have a place to stay. That night something terrible happened in that small house. We were all awakened from our sleep, because the dog of these people, tied to a long running wire, barked horribly, and we immediately thought of partisans. My mother and I tore open a small window and crawled in the darkness straightaway outside. We were not dressed. We didn't do that because of the fear that someone might catch us. We crawled as quietly as we could past the back wall of the house and made our way into the field. We stayed there until the next morning and couldn't see what was happening in the house. When we came back to the small yard, the woman lay in front of the house, where there was a small veranda; she was weeping loudly leaning over her dead husband. He looked awful. The Russian partisans had rubbed his whole back with a grater from the household of the woman and then strewed salt on it having tied his mouth so that he couldn't scream. The poor man had been painfully executed. The dog lay on his master and howled constantly. My mother and I, we sat beside that woman and all three of us were stunned in view of so much cruelty. My mother was the first to attend the woman. They carried the man into a little barn, laid him on a white cloth, and then the woman went to the nearest house in the neighbourhood. The houses were all far apart, and one had to cover at first a long distance to get to them. We stayed in the house and looked after two small children who were so intimidated that they were just only whimpering without stopping. Then the grieving woman came back with one woman and two men and we left the house as fast as we could. Someone could betray us.

We immediately went back the way we had come along the day before and hid ourselves away for a while, because we had found out that the whole area was full of partisans. Later, we went to the river Memel and always walked along it, where many fishermen's cottages stood. We also had more protection in this area by the waterside overgrown with shrubs and hedges. Sometimes, we could also boat with fishermen. Then the fish were cleaned by us, and people then hung them in smokehouses. If we were lucky, we also got some as a gift. Then, that was like Christmas for us. When we begged, we got mostly a piece of home-baked bread and a tin pot of milk. That was our staple food, and we were very, very thankful for that. The bread tasted like cake. It was always so nice juicy in taste. People baked it differently. Potato was often used for this. I often saw how the loaves were put into their own clay ovens and were laid on cabbage and reed leaves, so that they tasted good. Everyone had their own recipe for this, and it always tasted differently.

When we stayed with people for a day or two, I often had to work with my mother. I had then always to sprinkle dung on the field, to bind sheaves, to plough with a wooden plough, to turn hay and to heap it in heaps, to load horse driven carts with hay or grain. I also draw horses to handle the threshing machines, and those who did not have them beat the sheaves with flails on linen pieces or sacks and then cleaned the grain on sieves. That was really a hard work for a child of eleven years. Nevertheless, we were glad that we got something to eat by doing so. So we were on the move every day like vagabonds and didn't know at all where we were. We were like animals that had no orientation.

One thing we couldn't do at all was to go into a city, because then the Russians would have immediately captured and transported us away. Where, nobody knew. It was summer, and sometimes we bathed in the river Memel, because there was no other way to clean our bodies. We had only that, what we were wearing on our bodies and we stole some pieces of our clothing from the clotheslines hanging in peasant farmsteads, if no one noticed. We undressed, rubbed our bodies with sand, and plunged into water to rinse it off. My mother, who was a very good swimmer, also used to swim in the Memel, and since she sometimes plunged into a strong current and swam out somewhere else on the other riverbank, I was afraid that she might sink. But she always came back. Sometimes, I went to the sandbanks, over little dams that had been put up by the fishermen, and swiped gull eggs. Very often, we also used to empty chicken nests in barns, when we stayed there for the night. We did everything covertly. The raw eggs gave us strength to survive.

Between longing, fear and misery

One day, we were allowed to stay for a few days with a fisher family and also to sleep in a barn. My mother got a terrible nightmare that night and screamed loudly. I shook her to and fro, but it didn't help. I ran to the fisherman, rapped on the window glass and said he should come quickly. My mother was totally exhausted from screaming, and the man slapped heftily her face. Then she came to herself and flew totally pale-faced into the hay. The next morning she lay dead and was unable to get up. It wasn't until late in the afternoon as she came into the house and told us what she had experienced. It was a terrible dream about her children left behind in Königsberg. I was so shocked at it that I kept saying to my mother, "Mum, let's go back to Kaunas. We'll try to get back from the train station."

We footed it for quite some time, only the dear Lord knows where, but we were not approaching Kaunas, as if we were always running in a circle. Often we were back, where we had been already. But at some point, we started heading in the right direction, and we met a lot of begging children, they all were from East Prussia and had no parents.

One day, we met a woman, it was my aunt Lise, my father's sister who was in Königsberg a short while ago and managed to get away after her two children had starved to death. The children, like many others, had been buried in a mass grave. Lise was with her nerves at the end and totally emaciated. She was now begging for survival on her own. Now she told my mother that she no longer needed to go to Königsberg, because she knew perfectly well that my siblings Herbert, Hans, and Eva were dead. They had died of hunger in recent weeks and no one knew where they had been taken. Frau Neumann, who was supposed to take care of them, also died of hunger. That's what the people who lived in the house said. The world collapsed for my mother. She started shouting at my aunt repeatedly saying, "Lise, that's not true. Tell me. Is that really true?"- "I know for sure, Asta. You can believe me." I had been hollowed out and was just only crying. For days, over and over again. I couldn't believe that I wouldn't see my siblings again. Suddenly, I had no feeling for my mother anymore. I said to her, "Mum, why did you leave the siblings in Königsberg?" I couldn't understand it. I think, a bit of me died inside. I no longer had the desire to live and was marked by sadness. My aunt recognized that and stayed with us for a while.

We went back into the country's interior and had to beg. My mother became mentally ill, I think. She hardly spoke about it. We dragged ourselves through the countryside. Every day somewhere else. One day, my aunt broke away from us, because she had got sick. We were very fortunate that one family, where we begged for food, realized how sick she was and decided to take her until she would be well again. But my mother and I had to move on.

Hermitage

At some point, we came to the edge of a forest and saw a totally squalid hovel nearby. When we entered it, we noticed that no one lived in it, but it had been empty since not so long ago. Everything was in its place and even a cow and two sheep, even a pig were still in the stable, but they didn't bestir themselves anymore. They didn't have anything, neither to eat nor to drink. My mother said that there had been partisans there and they had kidnapped the whole family. Who knows where to? At first, we tried to herd out the animals to the pasture; we couldn't do it with the cow anymore. I got some water from the house well. It was handled with a wooden rod and a bucket. I brought the bucket to the stable and gave it to the lying cow to drink. She just swallowed it like that. An entire bucket was empty in no time. My mother brought the cow freshly plucked grass. It also ate it up, and it took a long time for the cow to get up and then we took it to the meadow near the house. Then we tethered all the animals so that they could eat in peace, and so we had brought them out of their misery. My mother and I stayed there for a few days. At night, we slept in the woods fearing the partisans. We had also found blankets in the house and could cover ourselves with them.

On the third day, we were very shocked when suddenly a man came into the wooden house and said to us that he was a neighbour. He didn't notice that the people had been gone. He had seen the animals in the meadow and now wanted to know what was going on. He was friendly to us and said we could stay, but we had to be very careful about the Russian controls. They were systematically having a look-see there. We had found some food in the house and milk we could get from the man in the neighbourhood. As we went there one day, a cow gave birth to a calf, but it was dead. He offered the meat to us and said we could still eat it, but would have to boil the meat out, if we wanted it. My mother helped with the skinning and he cut it for us. He also took off the innards. We put the pieces of meat in the bucket and then boiled them in salted water. It was a feast for us because we hadn't eaten meat for a long time and had a gorgeous meal on that occasion.

As one day we saw again someone approaching the house, we got very scared trying to make out what that would mean to us. It was a girl from East Prussia, 17 or 18 years old. She was totally emaciated and could barely walk. She was very happy having met Germans. She had two more siblings left. They had died of hunger while fleeing to Lithuania, and they had been left behind somewhere in the ditch. The parents had been already dead. Her mother had died from rape, and her father had been killed in action. It was bad for this girl. My mother said we had found enough food here: flour, potatoes and milk from the neighbour. We spent a few more days there. At night we were always in the woods.

But then, the Lithuanian came back to us and said, we should rather be going on again. It would be better for us. We packed up something edible and started footing it. We had spent almost 14 days there and were very happy. We also washed our things, which we had on, with real homemade hard soap and were again clean washed from head to toe. But we had fleas anyway. They bothered us. Everywhere we had flea bites, and if we scratched them, we got bumps everywhere and they itched horribly.

Always only onwards

The three of us went forth through the country, but it didn't last long. After about ten days, we parted again, because it was difficult for the three of us to procure something edible; nobody took us to stay overnight, because it was too dangerous for the people. We never saw the girl again.

My mother and I ran around the country every day never knowing what would be in store for us. We also had no idea if it was a weekday or Sunday. We only noticed when the Lithuanians went to the churches that were always full. These people are a deeply religious folk. Every little wooden hut had a small altar somewhere in a corner, where people prayed at least three times a day.

One day, we were looking for an overnight stay. It was a very cold day and I was weak in my legs. We had already asked several people for a place to stay, but everyone refused to keep us. The people were afraid of the Russians who drove around at night and searched all houses for Germans. We were desperate and I didn't realize that it was already very late and I got frozen to the marrow. We were cutting across country, and I had run against a barbed wire fence in the dark. Thereby I tore both my knees totally open. We had no bandages and couldn't see anything. The next morning, after spending the night at the edge of a forest between pines and bushes, I was blood-smeared and had a pain. We noticed a small house nearby. We went there and asked the people, if they could help to treat my knees. They let us in and came to me with a bottle in hand. When opened, it smelled really terrible. It was alcohol, and the woman washed my bloody knees with that. It hurt terribly, but I clenched my teeth. Then I got a makeshift bandage and was deeply grateful for the good deed. The people were very nice and kept us for a few days, but we had to spade potatoes in the field for that.

Four days later, we were again on the road, and I struggled

to move my knees. But I had no choice, we had to go on. It was getting colder afield, and we didn't have proper warm clothing to wear for the season. I decided to get it somehow and told my mother we had to steal something. Then I started watching out for what was hanging on the clotheslines when people had a wash. But it was very difficult to come nearer to the clothes. After a long lookout I managed anyhow to snitch some underwear for mother and me. On our feet we wore footwraps with felt covers. Sometimes we also took paper instead of it. It was also not so bad; the legs were warm then. Once we came to an area, where there were many orchards, and the fruit tempted us to stop there for a while. We found a place to stay nearby; this was a fairly robust shelter on a pasture at the edge of the forest. We settled in it and first ate apples and pears as much as we wanted. There were a few cottages nearby, and I went there to beg. People gave me some bread and some potatoes. We baked potatoes on fire, and it felt as if it were peace. But that was not the case. We had to keep on moving, couldn't stay longer. Some day we came to a place, where one man kept bees; beehives and baskets were scattered all over the fields. The man also took us in for a few days and for that we had to harvest turnips in small fields and load a box cart with full wicker baskets casting them up. It was a pretty hard job for me, but we went out of our way only to be able to stay overnight. We slept in the cowshed. It was always so nice and warm there at night. As three days later we came back to the field to harvest turnips, I was attacked by a swarm of bees and I had many bee stings on my face as well as on my body and looked terrible. I screamed in pain and ran around wildly. The man from that little house came to me with all the cooling things and applied everything to my face, but it didn't help. I looked awful.

After a few days, we moved on again and I went to one house to beg for something. There I saw an open home-made chest in a corner. There were many leather shoes in it. I grabbed a pair from it, which could be about my size and only then noticed that an old man slept on an old wooden bench in the room. I didn't think long and went quickly out of the house. My mother talked to a woman standing near the cottage. I took a different route and then stood on the beet field. My mother came to me and I tried on the stolen shoes at the first. They were too big for me, but that didn't matter. I tore off a piece from the old footwraps and stuffed the toe full. Then I put on the shoes and didn't have wet feet anymore.

Through Lithuania

At some point, my mother begged off a pair of wooden slippers. They were carried there by almost all people, and they made them themselves too. The men always sat around carving things out of wood. Slippers, wooden spoons, and soup plates were made from it. Women and young girls were making wool and linen into yarn. All things were woven and sewn out of this or very beautiful stylish Norwegian sweaters were knitted. I watched it all and wanted to do it too. Many people also allowed me to try it. I really enjoyed handling the spinning wheel, and the sheep wool was the easiest to spin, because the wool always felt so greasy. I didn't like to weave linen. It was hard and I always cut my fingers when I pulled the strings. But I did all the work the people gave. My mother wasn't apt to do that.

I also learned the Lithuanian language very quickly. My mother wasn't able to cope with it and had great difficulties. In the meantime, I could speak Russian and also quite good Lithuanian. The Lithuanians spoke only secretly their national language. We had been told that at the command of the Russians, they had to learn and speak Russian as the official language. But they had never abandoned their strict Catholic faith. They always attended church, whenever they could. On warm days they walked barefooted just to spare the shoes. Only in front of the church did they put on their shoes again because they might have had only one pair. There were a lot of poor people. Every little family that had a goat or a cow also had a centrifuge to make their own cream, butter or buttermilk. I often had to spin the crank of the butter churn. Then I took the opportunity and sometimes put a small bit of not yet skimmed butter in my mouth. That was delicious. The people made a lot of dishes from potatoes. They had a potato bread and potato cakes. Everything tasted good. I also saw how people cold-pressed oil out of poppy and flax seeds, and the remaining hard pieces were then dissolved in milk and given to small calves as a nutritional supplement. That was a delicacy for them.

The people were self-sufficient in every way. I don't know where my interest in all that came from. My mother shook it all off. But many people were so poor and couldn't give us anything, because they didn't have anything themselves. They were raided on by the Russians and partisans and had to give up everything they had. The Russians fetched everything in the night. That was always the case, and I knew it from Königsberg. We came to a family who asked us, if we wouldn't mind working in the field for a few days. We accepted it gratefully and were really happy. All day long I had to scatter dung that the farmer had driven onto the field some days before. My mother went with the farmer's wife to gather potatoes, which the man had dug up with a wooden plough. The following Sunday, we had to go to church with them sitting on a small carriage. They had harnessed a cow. They didn't have horses.

A little human being

When we were about half an hour away, we saw a child lying in a ditch. We all got off the cart and realized that it was a German begging child. It looked awful, totally exhausted and maybe five or six years old. The Lithuanian woman and my mother took carefully the child up to the car, and then we drove back to the family's home. My mother said to the woman who could also speak a little bit of German, she would like to prepare hot water, so that we could clean up the poor child first. The little one had the whole body covered with cockroaches' itches and lice, which would have soon eaten up that poor human being. Looking at it I couldn't help thinking about my brother Herbert. Now we all acted very fast. The woman put a zinc tub in the room, and then my mother put the little girl in the water, so that everything would become soft. The lice swarmed around the small body in masses, and it didn't become less, even after repeated water baths in the tub. My mother took a pair of scissors then and cut off the child's totally matted hair. The whole skull was a single scab crust, under which the lice were sitting. The girl lay totally exhausted in the tub and hardly spoke a word. We asked her name and where she had lived, but she couldn't tell us that. The woman was so sad about it that she could only cry. The man took all the things from the girl and set with alcohol fire to everything in the yard. When we had her rather clean, we put her in a dry cloth. The woman rubbed some cream into the body of the girl and she definitely felt like born again after that. Then the woman laid the nameless child into warm bed, and it fell asleep immediately. It didn't eat anything, but milk drank without end.

It had been an exhausting day for us; we couldn't understand how such a child had survived. But we were all overjoyed having saved the life of that small being. It was a coincidence that we just came by and found it, because the roads, which looked like field cart tracks, were used only by a few people. There were no cars at all, only the Russians got some, driving sometimes somewhere. The next morning, the girl woke up and was very scared. The woman and my mother put on her too big clothing that the woman had. There were also still lice on her body, which came down from the head. A week later, the girl also started to talk, and we learned from her that she had a brother and he might have left her there in the ditch, because she couldn't walk any longer. They had lost their parents in Königsberg who had died of hunger and they had been taken by a woman to Lithuania. The woman then abandoned the children and moved on alone. Tears were in my eyes. I was so sad, because I had to think about my own siblings and just only kept crying to myself. My mother asked, what was the reason for that, but I said nothing.

The girl was recovering very well and the woman said we had to go now, because they did not have so much food for all of us and it was dangerous for them to keep us. The little girl was to stay with them forever. We were so glad that the little girl had found her home, and she would also get a name. My mother and I thanked the hospitable family for having us and then we moved on again.

Daily drama

Now our daily drama went off again; we didn't know, whether we would get enough food begging or find a stay for the night. It was also getting colder afield and the days were getting shorter. If it was possible, we stayed in barns. It was rather not too bad for us there. But we had to take care that the watch dogs didn't get scent of us. We tried to get in mostly through back entrances. And often we had to take to our heels, because of the dogs. There were enough people tracking us down in the barns and then chasing us away. Then there were some who allowed us to stay for the night in their stables. We liked to sleep in there. The animals gave off a lot of heat, and we felt comfortable. Towards winter, people didn't muck out the stalls at all. That remained in the stable until spring. Some fresh straw was put on it every day, and animals had a warm shed. After a while, I said to my mother, "How long should we carry on so? Every day we have to worry about our overnighter. What if the Russians catch us somewhere?" Mother said, that then they will certainly abduct us and bring to Siberia like others. I always panicked when I thought it could be like this. "Mum," I said, "then I'll kill myself first, but not to Russia!"

I couldn't simply get over what had happened in Königsberg. I suffered terribly, and only because we were somewhere else every day and always had different faces around us, I was a little bit distracted from it. But when it was calm around me, the pictures were back, and I was brooding over everything I had experienced. And there was nobody who could help me. My mother never talked much about it. I think her soul had completely died out. Somehow, she had become a sick woman. A quite different one than before. We both didn't have a mother-child relationship anymore. I felt like a totally adult person, because as a small child I had to go through so many bad things. I thought sometimes about my life, if I possibly had to go to school as an eleven- or a twelve-year-old. I could neither read, nor write, nor calculate. I was absolutely good for nothing. Not even my mother tongue was correct. This came about, because we didn't even get in touch with Germans anymore. Only Lithuanian was spoken. I could speak it better and better, but my mother couldn't. That's why I always had to beg people for everything.

Shelter for labour

At some point, after weeks, we came to a small farm, and the family wanted to keep us for some time, but only if we would go each day to the forest to cut wood and then saw it. Somehow we were glad to have a place to stay for a while, because winter was approaching and it was bitterly cold. We were well received by the people. We got milk and bread when we drove into the woods with the farmer and his two sons. It was an ox cart that took us there every day. It was awfully cold, but we clenched our teeth and held on. There were only birches and pines in the forest, and only the birch trees were felled. My mother and I then sawed the felled trees to pieces with a whipsaw. That might have been tormenting us mercilessly, but we had nothing else to do in our plight. When it was evening and we drove back to the farm, we were so broken that we could hardly eat our soup. It was like that for about three weeks, but then we couldn't stand it anymore and sneaked away one night.

We milled around trying to get a room for the night, and one family took us there. They had four children. I was really happy to be able to talk to children in Lithuanian. One of the children was a blind boy, and he wanted to know everything about who I was and where I came from. Then I told him that I was a German beggar, and he couldn't grasp it. His mother then told everything again, but it was too hard for him to understand. He was the same age as me. There we stayed for a week and were very happy there. My mother helped the woman with the laundry, and I helped in the kitchen when butter was made or when bread was baked. Then I shaped the loaves. They had a clay oven, and bread was baked in there. Stoves of such kind were almost in every house. When the bread was taken from the oven and the scent was spreading in the room, our mouths were watering. After the bread had cooled down, all children were the first to be treated with a piece of it and with a tin pot full of fresh milk.

I felt very comfortable in this family and was very sad when we had to move on again in the great cold. I was lucky that the woman gave me a warm cotton quilted jacket that was from her kids. I even got knitted socks and gloves from her. I flung my arms around her neck out of sheer joy, and we both cried. I told her, maybe next year we would come back and visit her. We could do that, she said. We children had become friends, and my mother had got along well with the woman. The man could also speak a little bit our language. He had been in Germany once. We often thought of this dear family after my mother and I moved around again.

But we were always lucky this winter that someone took us in for a day or two. But people always had to be very careful not to be caught by the Russians, otherwise it could be very bad for them. But in the freezing cold, the Russians didn't do the searches in the houses too often. We also had sometimes an opportunity to stay in a church and spend a night there. They were often open and that was lucky for us. Now in the winter, less people came in and the Russians didn't at all. We noticed everything. By moving constantly, we were braving the great cold around us. We also got hardened and could withstand coughs and sneezes. The hot milk we begged each day did our bodies good.

After wandering around for a few weeks, we returned to the Memel river area and were taken in by a fishing family. The Memel was frozen and had a thick layer of ice. I went on it and shovelled out a really smooth ice rink. The people had two daughters about the same age as me, and we quickly made friends. We played together on that smooth and slippery ice. During our stay with these people I was also able to enjoy a warm bath sitting in a bath trough. That had been only a dream of mine before. I felt like a king in this environment. They were very nice to us. My mother tried to learn how to weave, but she didn't succeed in all that. I also did it and found it very enjoyable. I was also allowed to work at the spinning wheel and to spin sheep wool.

That was the work people did the whole winter. I wanted to learn everything and they showed me; my mother often shook her head in surprise. I also learned the Catholic prayers and songs when people spoke or sang. Then they were always pleased to see that a German begging child accepted their customs and traditions. After a few days we had to take leave of the family and foot it again. We promised to come there again in summer, if we would manage it. The woman had given me another big sweater and a linen skirt. My mother had received a thick wool cardigan from the woman. That was a big help in the cold.

Now we asked for shelter every night, because if we stayed

afield, we would have caught frostbites for sure. That would have been bad for us. The people also understood our situation and helped us, even if it was just a stable. Day after day, we had nothing else but to struggle for our survival. We always had to see to it that there was a fresh meal for us to stay active. The daily cold didn't always make it easy for us to walk, and we made our way into the woods and then sat huddled in the thicket or under fir trees.

A bit of sun

Now, it was slowly moving towards spring, and the sun gave us the warmth we needed to face the day. From time to time, we also saw a farmer in the field who was putting in order his little plot of land. Then we watched people going into the birch woods; they picked out particular birch trees and put small tubes in their trunks. The holes had been previously drilled out in the trunk with a hand drill. Then the birch sap dropped into containers set up below. When containers were full, they were taken home and wooden barrels were filled with it. As soon as they had enough birch sap, the wood ash from their ovens was added to it; and that had to ferment for some time. Then they had handy lye that was used to wash hands. Useful things were made out of simple ingredients, and it always worked. Only the need brings us to it.

Now, people took us in easier again, because they could use us for some field work. Mostly it was to muck the stables out or to scatter dung on some field for hours and hours. Then everything was ploughed up with a wooden plough pulled by oxen or horses. We also laid potatoes in the furrow and earthed them up. It was a hard job for me to drug all the time a self-woven wicker basket full of potatoes behind me. When we were in the fields, we had to be very careful not to be caught. The Russians drove everywhere along, but reluctantly avoided the fields, because the partisans could be entrenched there. We also had to take care of the Lithuanians who were good disposed to the Russians. Then we could have been lost for sure.

Sometimes, we were turning around in circles. Since we had no timepiece, we felt like lost children and had no sense of time. The sun was our clock. We got used to orient ourselves according to it. Most of the time, we stayed near the forests. Because we could always disappear there immediately, if we felt to be endangered. Now, towards the summer, we again met many partisans, and we suspected that there were more and more of them. They had dug their shelters in the woodlands under the forest floor. Sometimes, when we met some of them at the edge of the woods, they told us not to betray them, no matter whom. We were very scared and didn't tell anyone. The people were afraid of Russian raids at night and more and more sought the partisans' protection. Thus, the atrocities on both sides also increased. But we were really indifferent to all that. It didn't bother us anymore when we witnessed it and looked at the dead.

But for all that, the Lithuanians had to till their fields or to harvest. It all happened with mixed feelings, because they always lived in fear, something could happen. From time to time, we were asked by some people, whether we wanted to help with hay drying or to plant potatoes. We were always looking forward to coming across a place to be able to stay there for a few days.

Now, the time of the year was on our side. Because when it got warmer afield, we could sleep outdoors. We lay down to sleep under small haystacks on meadows. But most of all, we liked to stay under protection of the fir-trees thicket. It was dense and dark there, neither the Russians nor the partisans could see us. So we batted around almost the whole country, always tramping and coming to a different area, and there were always German children to see everywhere, totally neglected, relying on themselves alone. People called us starving wolf kids from East Prussia, and they were completely right. We simply were not anything else.

Forever in a circle?

Now, the autumn was inevitably in store for us, and terrible thoughts about the approaching winter were hunting us. My mother and I had been heading for the Memel. We had been footing it for weeks until we reached it again. We could clean ourselves properly in the water. We went to the fishermen's houses situated far afield, begged and sometimes got to eat a smoked fish. The small fishing boats went out daily to catch something. They also made small wicker baskets for trapping fish and set fishing nets. Once, I was lucky to be allowed to boat and was very excited. In the past, I was allowed to go with, when my uncle Karl fished coal in the harbour; the cranes had lost it, when they loaded barges in the harbour basin.

We stayed near the river until late autumn and so made ends meet. Once we were able to stay with a fishermen's family for almost two weeks, because they needed us to weave wicker baskets that they wanted to sell in Kaunas. I was also allowed then to go to Kaunas. It went on like this: We were taken by a rowboat to the steamer, which stopped in the middle of the river Memel. The paddle steamer couldn't come ashore, because the Memel has many sandbanks. For me it was an adventure that I enjoyed to the fullest. We had taken a few baskets and some smoked fish. All this was swapped in the market. We took home a lot of salt with us. This was traded like gold. Everything for everyday use was in short supply. People also had to see how they could get the goods.

Then we were unprotected birds again and went day in and day out around the area and asked ourselves, when all this would have an end for us. Actually, we were worse off than animals. They could be brought back to the stable in the evening, because it was getting colder from then on, but we were exposed to all kinds of weather and nowhere at home. This thought made me sometimes so sad that I didn't want to go on any further. At some point, I just stopped and said to my mother, "Mum, why do we have to go through all this? I didn't do anything. Why must all the people in Konigsberg starve and freeze to death?" Then we both cried terribly, and my mother couldn't tell me anything more.

I was really scared, because now the cold winter was coming back and we didn't know if we would survive it. People no longer dared to accept the Germans, because they were severely punished for that. The deportation to Siberia daunted them. We again moved to hinterlands and sought shelter in the woods. We still found sometimes a few potatoes on harvested fields. We baked them on stones then. That was a pleasure for us. There wasn't much fruit. An apple or a pear, here and there. I was always happy, when I spotted a cow somewhere in a pasture. Then I ran there and milked the tin pot full of milk. They didn't always like it and kicked hard with their hind legs. I fled then lightning-quick. My mother didn't dare to approach the cows. Sometimes a pig was slaughtered somewhere and we were really happy when we got a tin pot full of broth or a bit of bacon. But that was a total exception.

Now it was already dark, and we footed it to houses, where a glimmer of light appeared, hoping to get a place to stay for the night. But mostly we got a refusal. The people were just scared. But we might have made such a miserable impression that some took us into a stable or a barn. But very often we had nothing else but to cling to each other and spent the night in a fir trees thicket, and early in the morning we stood stock-still up and jumped around to warm us up again. To add to that, we had no real clothes, and now we had to look out again for something we could have on in cold winter days, and even if it would be stolen from some clothesline again.

One day, my mother was approached by a man standing on a road. She didn't understand what he wanted. I said to Mum that he asked, if we would like to join him. We were very cautious and said no. I felt ill at ease about this and we got quickly away. I suddenly got very scared and I said, "Mum, let's hasten away, as far as it goes. So, that he wouldn't be able to chase us." Until evening we had run several kilometres for sure. As we began to ask for an overnight, we told one woman what had happened to us, and that we were still scared. Then the woman, perhaps a little older than my mother, said that may be it was a Russian who wanted to lure us somewhere to rape my mother. She had heard that a number of Lithuanian women had been violated recently, and their men had been abducted. Everyone was afraid of the night-time raids carried out by Russian soldiers. It was an area that wasn't suitable for ust at all, and we went away the next day. We tried to hide out as much as possible, whenever we saw anyone. We were very lucky. Nothing happened to us.

What with have we deserved this?

In the evening, we met a German begging girl who was also about my age, but she didn't speak much German anymore. We talked in Russian, she could do that better than Lithuanian, and she said that she would like to wander about alone. Her mother had been raped by Russian soldiers and later died. Her father had been killed in the war, and she had also left Königsberg a few months ago.

We parted then again, and each went their own way. Later, I said to my mother, "Mum, why didn't we ask the girl if she would like to go with us?" – "That would be too dangerous for all of us. Nobody would take us then anymore." Again we had to take care of an overnight stay, because it was already getting cold, but I thought of that poor human child. Where would she sleep that night?

Then we saw a light shimmering in the distance and headed determined towards it. The dog that was tied up with a long chain had already got scent of us and barked like crazy, and then a male voice answered. I said that we were Germans and asked for a night's lodging. He thought first, and then he said we could come in. We were ushered into a small wooden house, and there sat four children, a woman, as well as grandfather and grandma. They asked where we came from and gave us food. We were overjoyed to be under a roof. They had a high clay oven. All children crawled up there to sleep. There was also a small chamber there. The grandfather and the grandma took themselves off to bed there. The man and the woman fetched two puffed up straw sacks. They lay down on one of them in the middle of the room, and we placed the other in the corner. We lay down with all the clothing we had on our bodies. The next morning the man woke us up early and told us to leave. They were afraid that maybe Russians were around and could conduct controls. We got another piece of bread and some milk to drink and then we left very early and noticed how cold it was already afield.

In the following days we were lucky. We had discovered a pasture shed again. There were no more cows in the pasture, so we hogged it right away. We brought dry twigs from the nearby forest, and there was still some straw in the hut. In this way, the night lodging was made for a few days. During the day we moved around, and in the evening we crawled in the hut and lay close together. The main thing was that we didn't have to lie outside. But I was always scared because of the partisans or Russians. They would have carted us off, right away. In the meantime, my mother and I met a family who gave us a pair of self-made socks. That was really great to have again really warm feet in our wooden clogs. From a clothesline I was able to get hold of a green linen skirt and a headscarf for my mother. She was very happy about it as she got it. Sometime later, I received a sweater as a gift knitted like a Norwegian one. Well, that was just what! I could hardly believe it, and it was so nice and warm! We stayed until the first snow fell. We had to move on then, because we didn't get anything from the people anymore, because we came every day to them to beg. They simply couldn't bear us standing and begging in front of them anymore.

Now, as the snow was everywhere and the cold came, it was the worst time for us and all other begging children. Every day just turned into a fight for survival. What with have we deserved this? We felt like rats, always on the run from anything. People also got tired of us, because more and more people were wandering around the country. The Lithuanians themselves didn't have much and were constantly robbed by the Russians and partisans. The battles between them didn't stop either. We couldn't understand why it was like this. We didn't know anything about the rest of the world, or what was going on outside of Lithuania, or if there was anything else besides Lithuania. Years, months, days or a sense of time didn't exist for us. We were just no more people, just wolf kids who were moving in a circle or milling around. Sometimes I said to my mother, "Mum, what's going to happen to us? I can neither read nor write, I don't know anymore how to count and to speak German properly." – "I also don't know how that will end. If we all just died, we wouldn't have to experience it anymore." We footed it often crying and were sometimes at the end, but then we pulled ourselves together again.

As we were wandering around, we noticed that more and more trucks with Russian soldiers drove along very bad country roads. My mother used to say that they have something to do with the people who live in the area; and in fact we heard from some people that they had taken many men away from their families, and no one knew where they had been taken to. We got scared and didn't know where we had to go. Then, as so often, we passed a forest and noticed that the partisans were living there. They approached us and asked where we came from and who we were, and whether we had seen many Russians in recent days. They told us to get out of this area. There could be some fighting, and it would be dangerous for us. We followed the advice and got out far away. In the evening, we were so broken that we could barely walk. We went to a small wooden house and asked for an overnight stay. An elderly couple went with us to a small stable.

There were three pigs and a few sheep in it. We were allowed to lie down in a corner and sleep. Overjoyed, we fell into the corner. It was so nice with the animals. We liked most of all to sleep like this in winter. The animals gave off so much heat. If there was also a cow or a goat somewhere, we also had milk as well. During milking, I put the udder's teat into my mouth and so drank the warm milk. We were also happy about a chicken nest full with fresh eggs. They were cracked by us right away and drunk raw. That gave us a lot of strength. I can't remember that we had ever needed a doctor. We had endured everything.

We were allowed to stay for a few days with the people who had taken us in, but they didn't take us into the house for fear that someone could see them hosting Germans. We spent the whole day in the barn and helped a bit dumping muck out of the barn and scattering straw. Most of the time, we slept and rested for the days to come, when we would have to go out into the cold again. My mother got an old jacket and a sweater from the woman. It was a great gift, and my mother was very happy about it. For me she had a pair of self-made mittens. It was wonderful to have warm hands while wandering around. Otherwise I rubbed my icy hands with snow when they were tingling because of the cold. The fingers were aching sometimes so unbearably. We were very sad by the time we had to leave that family, but that was just the way it was.

One day, it must have been Sunday, because people went or went by horse-drawn sleighs to church, we discovered that the church door in the next village was open. So we snuck in and hid ourselves in a dark corner. Nobody had seen us. My mother said the church would be surely open for a few hours, and we could stay in it as long as that. A pastor came to the church in the evening and we crawled out on all fours.

Finally a place to stay

The dry cold cut mercilessly through our bodies. It scrunched underfoot as we roamed around. One day, we came to an area, where there was a windmill and four houses at long intervals, all built of wooden beams. We went to it to beg for something edible for us. One family took us and ushered into the only large room, where we were given a hot meal. But we had to say a prayer in Lithuanian beforehand. When we had eaten our meal, we went off again, because people had ordered it so. I wanted to go to the windmill and see it all.

We came there; a man came towards us and asked, where we wanted to go. We told that we had been walking around for a long time and couldn't bear anymore to be afield in the cold. It looked, as if he had great compassion for us and first took us into the mill. He then left for a while, and we stayed alone. We got scared and wanted already to leave. But then we saw that the man was approaching us with a woman from the house. They were very friendly to us, and so we also confided in them at once. He asked my mother, if I could stay with them. I translated it to my mother in German, and she got at first very much startled and said nothing at all. I, on the other hand, was so happy to stay there that I said, "I want to stay here, Mum. Leave me here. You can always come here and see how it is with me. Please, please, I don't want to go begging anymore. I stay here." I don't know what had occured to me, but I decided myself and stuck with it. My mother saw it and let it happen. They took us into the house. It had a room, where everyone lived, and there was a large clay oven inside it with a setup, where people could sleep on. Then, there was a small hall, and there were also two small rooms next to it, all with homemade furniture. It was cosy anyway. I was allowed to behold everything and the man said that the smallest room was for me and my mother could stay here for a few days. But from then on I wasn't permitted to speak German anymore, but always only Lithuanian or Russian. I didn't care about all that. The main thing, I could stay there.

Suddenly, I had a place to stay. I couldn't believe it. We also got a nice, warm meal at first. It was a potato dish and tasted great. My mother slept with me in the room on a straw bag lying on the ground. However, I could sleep for the first time in a bed from olden times, which also had a straw bag on. In addition I got a woollen blanket to cover up. First, I washed myself properly with water and curd soap and noticed that my body was pricked all over by flea bites. I had thick wheals everywhere from scratching the skin. My mother was also able to wash herself properly. We then fell into a deep sleep. At night, I heard a miserable cry from inside the house. I got very scared and awoke my mother from her dream. She also listened to that and said to me, it sounded like young cats. She walked out of the room, and in fact there were five new-born cats behind our door. We left them there, and the next morning I could admire them. They couldn't see yet. That came a few days later. I then fed them every day with milk that I got milked each morning and evening from two cows. The work in the stable became my main job from now on and I did it with a huge joy.

My mother stayed there for a few more days and worked a little bit, and then she had to go on a begging tour, all by herself. We took leave of each other, and at first the separation between us wasn't hard for me. Mother promised to come over from time to time to see how I felt. I was very happy about that and had a very good feeling. The woman had supplied my mother with bread, bacon and milk. She also gave her a pair of old felt boots, a knitted skirt, and a thick scarf, so that her body was a little bit warmer in the biting cold.

A kind of everyday life

When she left and I watched her going away for a long time, I became very sad. I ran into the stable, sat down in a corner and started to cry terribly. Suddenly, the thought of my siblings struck me. It was very bad for me. I thought, now I was completely alone and didn't have anyone left. I wanted to run after my mother, but I pulled myself together and thought, then I would have to die someday, if we wouldn't get anything to eat. This thought had seized me so much that I got up and went into the house to join the people. They noticed that I had cried. Then the woman enfolded me in her comforting arms. She wanted to be good to me waving away my sad thoughts. The fear came over me, and I couldn't sleep the following night. I kept thinking, what's going to happen to me, if I would stay here forever.

The first few days were very hard for me, but over time I got used to everything, also that I had to work there. The man was almost always in the mill and had his job there. The woman and I did everything in the house and stable. She showed me all the household-related work as to how to make bread, knit stockings, weave fabrics, dye wool, spin wool and flax, and of course to keep the stable clean. But I really enjoyed learning it. I even had to be a helping hand during distilling of schnapps, and it was done only at night.

I also even witnessed some visits of Russians to them. The son of these people had Russian acquaintances and then it was always celebrated. The Russians didn't realize that I was a German child. The man had told them I was a relative of them. I spoke only Lithuanian and Russian, and they believed it. I had been there for a few weeks, as a pig was then slaughtered. In the morning, it was driven to the small yard, and a man living in the neighbourhood came to kill it; then it was put on its side to scorch it with burning straw tufts and to scald it with hot water. Afterwards, the bristles were scraped off. I could really eat as much of meat as I wanted.

I hadn't experienced anything like that in the last few years. I liked the meat broth most of all. Then everything was brined, so that it was durable. The woman always baked a very tasty potato cake. It was prepared with bacon greaves, boiled potatoes, onions, raw potatoes, salt, pepper, eggs and cream, and it was baked on a baking sheet in the oven. Sometimes there was a variation, and then she put everything in a saucepan. Then a piece of meat came in the middle, and it was cooked on a round hearth plate in the clay oven. Everything tasted very good. I always paid attention to how she did everything. When I cleaned the rooms, I took a small wooden bowl with water, dribbled it on the floor in the whole room so, that there would be no dust, and then swept up the dirt with a homemade birch broom. The floor had become really arched because of many sweepings in the course of years. The self-carved furniture stood already quite askew around the room.

Now, the cold season was setting in, and I always thought of my mother, if she would get a place to stay when evening arrived. I thought that she would definitely come at some point and take me back. But I didn't want to leave this place anymore. At last I felt again like a human being and wanted to push everything else to the back of my mind. But it didn't work, because I was always dreading it at night someone might take me away from here. Also, I was constantly thinking about my siblings trying to imagine how they probably looked like, when they starved to death.

A few weeks later, I got really sick from those bad thoughts. I didn't want to eat anymore, and people tried to cheer me up with a lot of encouragement. It didn't help much. My little soul was somehow struck. They also noticed that. I didn't feel like doing anything until someday people invited some young girls to join them. They came to us from the neighbouring houses and brought their spinning wheels, and then they all sat in the room. They started singing while spinning wool. The woman gave me a spinning wheel, and I was allowed to participate. I really liked it, and it was a great experience for me. At a late hour, they all even began to dance to the tune they sang. It looked weird to me, because they all wore wooden clogs and couldn't really spin around on the arched clay floor. Nevertheless, we all had fun. Now, they had all taken me in their circle of friends, and I was also allowed to go to them.

I didn't notice, how the weeks were going by. From time to time, we went to the forest full of birch-trees to get wood. For this, we took food for the whole day. Then I sawed through the tree trunks with the son of the family with a two-man saw and afterwards I was so broken that all my bones pained. A few days later, we took it out of the woods to the courtyard, with a cart driven by a horse. Then it was sawn into smaller pieces on a saw block and then I had for days to chop them on a chopping block and to stack the firewood. That was mostly my job. It was a backbreaking work for me, but I put up with everything just to stay there. I had daily food and drink and that was a huge fortune for me. On Sundays, I had almost always to go to a Catholic church that was fairly far off. The Lithuanians always tried to get there, although it was very difficult because of the Russian controls. Well, I also learned the prayers that were spoken daily before dinner. That was just a duty for all Lithuanians. From time to time, I also tried to write something in Lithuanian, but that didn't work, because the exercise in writing was gone. Sometimes I thought, how could it be further with me? I couldn't write anymore. All this had become a minor matter for us. The life-sustaining tasks had become very different. I had to fulfil my daily duties and was happy with it.

Now, it was time for spring, and the sheep that they had were let graze on the pasture. Before that, they were driven through a small pond in the yard to bathe and disinfect them. I had to muck the barn out, because the dung hadn't been cleared out of the barn during the winter months, because it gave off heat for the animals.

Meeting again and farewell

After a few weeks, at night, I heard a knock on the window of the room, where I slept. I was terribly scared and didn't move. I saw a shadow and recognized my mother in it; I bounced out of bed and opened the window. I saw that she was crying and asked, "Mum, what's wrong with you?" – "Ulla, let me in. I can't anymore." I ran to the woman and knocked on the door, where they slept. She came out and I said, my mother was outside and couldn't keep going. She and I went to her, picked her up and brought into the house. She was totally weakened and had been struggling along to reach us with the last of her strength. The night was over for all of us. Then the man came, and we all sat together. My mother took me in her arms and said, "Ulla, come with me." – "No, no!" I exclaimed in fear, "I stay here. You can stay here for the time being." So I begged the people to take my mother for a few days and hide her, so that she wouldn't be discovered when control came. I cried terribly for fear of having to leave again. Surely people felt so pity for my mother; they hugged her, and told me that she could stay here for a while, but only sleep in the stable. Both of us got filled with huge joy due to that.

First of all, my mother had to be well fed up. She was exhausted. I provided her with milk, bacon and everything we ate. But she wasn't allowed to appear outside. It was too dangerous for all of us. After three weeks she had recovered well, and then the man told her to move on again and asked me if, I wanted to go with. "No, I want to stay with you."

Now we had to say goodbye again, but hoping to see each other again soon. My mother got some clothes to wear from the woman, a pair of new wooden shoes and something to eat. I stood in front of the door and waved her for a long time until I couldn't see her anymore. Then I was overwhelmed with bitter grief. I threw myself on my straw bed and cried horribly. Suddenly, I was away from my mother again. For weeks I fought with it, until peace returned to me again.

The summer time was approaching us and I had to work a lot on the field. The hay had to be flipped over all the time, and then it had to be stacked, later it was transported with a cart to a small barn for drying up. Often, the son came with his Russian friends and then they made a real drinking bout with the father. I got then very much scared, ran to the barn or to the mill and hid myself away there for hours. Only when everyone was gone, I dared to come into the house. Sometimes, I thought, why didn't come any partisans here, when they have so many Russians here? The girls came also to us on several occasions and then in summer we sat in front of the wooden house and sang. It was really fun. They also did some needlework thereby. That was still too difficult for me. At that time, I could only knit stockings.

One day, a woman from the neighbourhood came highly excited to us and told that her husband had been taken away by the Russians who came to them at night and that he didn't come back. She had three children and poured out her heart to us asking to help them all. The miller went with her immediately and looked at the house. But the man never came back. In the next few weeks, such things happened again and again; in our area, people were taken away at night. Now the miller with his wife got scared, he told his son, he shouldn't bring the Russians anymore. I thought of my mother. Where is she likely to be? Maybe we two never get together again. But people calmed me down and said my mother would surely come before long.

The harvest was soon over. The grain was knocked out with flails in the barn. I also had to swing the flail together with the adults. It was a very hard job for me, but I had to go through it. The grain was then put into large, round sieves and the chaff was then removed from it by means of tossing the grain into the air on a windy day. The husks flew away and the grains stayed behind. They were then poured into jute sacks, and the miller brought them all to the mill to grind flour. It was the winter stock to bake bread. The miller's wife could also make good pastries from it; they were mostly filled with meat. I've often thought of trying it all myself, but it was too much for me. The work I had to do in the stable took a lot of strength and I was often very tired of it. But now autumn was setting in and the potato harvest was approaching. It was a great time for us all. I was particularly looking forward to it because then I could make a fire on the field and bake the fresh potatoes. That was a great thing.

My thoughts had always been, hopefully this time would never pass, and nobody would take me away from here. I was always scared of everything that I had experienced. After a few weeks the rumours went around that all beggar children were picked up and no one knew where they had been brought to. My anxiety was getting worse, and at night I often cried myself to sleep or hid myself among the animals in the stable. Nobody could comfort me either.

One night, the dog barked quite excitedly. I was overcome by fear, because the barking didn't stop. The miller left the house to see who was there; I opened the stable door, and recognized in the darkness my crying mother who was going to the house. My thought was, "Now I have to get out of here." She said, "Where is my daughter Ulla?" The man took her inside the house, then he came to see me, and a few minutes later took me to my mother. I felt, the good time was over for me. Well, as I was alone with my mother, I said to her, "Mum, I don't want to go away. I don't want to go begging again. Leave me here." We both stood weeping and I couldn't grasp, why we had become so strange to each other. The people stood in silence and didn't know what could be advised. My mother said, "Ulla, we have to get out of here. The Russian cars collect all Germans. I don't know what to do next." I kept begging, "Let me stay here." I didn't want to go, but my fight was lost.

'You Germansky?'

My mother took me in the morning, and I felt very unhappy, as never before. The people had provided us with food for a few days. My mother tried to comfort me, but I was far from her in my thoughts. I felt nothing at all and just thought, where we would be caught soon. We always tried to go over fields or country roads, just not to be captured. Since it was already cold afield, we couldn't sleep in the forest at night and begged for an overnight stay anywhere. People were more and more afraid to take us in, and I thought about the good time with the family. I often said to my mother, "Why haven't you left me there?" – "Ulla, that's impossible. We have to stay together, when they pick us up." I didn't care anymore.

A few days later, we went to a fir trees plantation to have a short rest and to eat the bread we had begged off before. Then we saw a truck behind us. The soldiers stopped and said, "You Germansky?" We knew, what was going to be now, and they ordered us to get up into the truck. We saw that many children were already crouching under the tarp and they all were terribly afraid. They all looked totally neglected, just like us, and nobody said a word. Next to them sat the guards and they watched that no one jumped down from the car. We drove and drove, and there was no end. Luckily, we still had some bread and milk with us and could maintain us with that. Towards evening, we drove into a city, and I realized that it had to be Kaunas.

We drove into the grounds of a former factory and saw that many people, but almost all children, were roomed in several empty halls there. We suddenly got scared and looked at each other wondering what would happen to us now. The car stopped in front of a hall and two Russian guards asked us to get off the truck. Everyone had to line up in rows. My mother was the only adult among us. We were counted and then led into a hall, where there were already many children and some women. They had no beds and no possibilities to sit down anywhere. They all were lying scattered on bare floors. It was an abject misery that we saw there. I started crying and said, "Mum, I want to go back to the family." My mother replied, "Ulla, there is no going back for us. Who knows what will happen to us now?" I was shaking with fear all over my body, and many children cried like me. It was terrible. The women told my mother, they had been there for a few days and no one knew what to do with us. We stayed there for about 14 days or three weeks. We couldn't make it out, because we had no sense of time, and because no one had a clock; we were like animals in a cage. Nobody got any information. It was very bad. We even heard that some people had committed suicide, because they believed that we all had to be taken to Siberia. Everything was so uncertain. We all were dozing in the dirt, received only thin water gruel and a piece of bread as a daily ration, and nothing else. There were no possibilities to wash ourselves somewhere or to go to the lavatory. This was done somewhere in corners and everything stank after that. We were in the grip of horrible circumstances.

Russia, Poland or Germany?

Then one evening, we all were tucked again in trucks, again guarded, and then we were driven in convoy through the streets to a goods railway station. There was a long freight train standing there and we all had to get in.

It took some time till we all were stuffed like cattle in waggons. All children got terribly scared and we burst out crying. The waggons were closed from outside, and a short time later the train began to move. My mother also cried and said to me, "Ulla, now we all come to Russia. I am very afraid for all of us." No one said anything, and there was also a strong cold around us. The rattle of the train pierced marrow and bone. There were no blankets. We only had our bare lives, and who knew how much longer. The ride didn't want to end, and no one could really fall asleep in the cold. My mother and I clung firmly together for the first time after a long, long time.

Suddenly, we took care of a jolt given by our train, and noted that it was the only one; the train stopped. Suddenly, we heard voices in Russian and thought we were in Russia. But that wasn't the case. We all had to get out of the waggons after they had opened the doors. It was a big freight yard, where bright lights shone on us. We all stood around and were blinded by the light. There was a strange unease among the guards, and then more of them came. They all had writing materials in their hands, and we thought, what was going to happen now? We all had to line up as far as space allowed, and now we were interviewed by an interpreter, as to how we were called, where we came from and how old we were. That took several hours. In the morning, I said to my mother, "Do you know, where we are?" It was Königsberg. However, we were not told that by our guards, because our trip had to go ahead further. We had to stay ignorant.

Then they ordered us to get into the waggons again. Everyone got a piece of bread and some water, nothing else. The doors were closed and even sealed off. We saw it as we looked through the small windows at the top of our waggon. Now everyone thought, we would be really brought to Russia, because they had registered all of us. The train started some time later, and this ride really wasn't going to end. So many days, we drove through the unknown landscapes, and no one could make out, where we were right now. When the train stopped somewhere, it was almost always a free stretch, where you couldn't see anything, and the bad thing was that nobody was allowed out. Everything was sealed off. We relieved ourselves in the waggon, in tin boxes, which some children still had with; they had drunk out of them before. This was then spilled out through a small peephole while the train was rolling on. It wasn't possible otherwise. We lay side by side like tree logs, suffering from cold and then – from hunger and thirst. They didn't give us anything during our ordeal. The fight for survival began for us again, and the last crumbs of bread that we had begged off in Lithuania were distributed among us. We had a woman with us in the waggon who got a very bad heart attack during our transportation, and nobody could help her. Everyone was at a loss. At some point, the woman had then recovered, and she lay totally exhausted on the bare wooden planks of the waggon foor. There was nothing to be covered with or to keep ourselves warm.

After four days, we stopped somewhere and saw that this was a railway station area with countless railroad constructions, and there were gardens nearby that we noticed immediately. We also saw vegetables in them and thought of nothing else now, except how to get these. We suddenly heard voices that didn't sound Russian. My mother said that could be Polish. They opened the sealed doors, and all people plunged like animals into the gardens near the railways. It went over fences, which were partially torn down, only to get to the cabbages, carrots and other edible things. I had discovered a house over the rails; I ran there to beg for something. Once there, I rushed to the very first house and knocked hard on the front door. A woman opened it and I spoke to her in Lithuanian, if she wouldn't have something for me to eat. She took me briefly into the house, and gave me a plate full of soup; I ate it greedy and went away quickly. She gave me quickly a 5-Zloty bill in the hand, and then I heard the whistle of our locomotive. I ran to the train as fast as I could, fell over a rail and bashed my left knee open. I thought, if the train gets under way I might have to stay here. The fear overwhelmed me, and I ran even faster. With great difficulty I reached the waggon; my mother was already there, and a short time later we drove on again until the next day. Then the train stopped at a place, where there was a big river. It should have been the Oder, and the day before we had a stop in Warsaw. We all were allowed to get out and rushed to the water to get rid of all the dirt that stuck to us in the train. We took water in washed tin cans for fear of not getting it again. When we were all in the waggons, women and men came; I think they were Poles. They had water in buckets and bread in baskets; that was distributed among us until the containers were empty; I don't think that everyone got something. But everything was then fairly divided in the waggon; and that was the first help we had. After hours, it went on again, and no one knew, where we were rolling to. It went into the night, and it was very cold. In our opinion, it might have been October or November. We didn't know what day or hour it was, the sun was our clock-hand. We had then discovered that our train passed through several towns and villages we had never seen or known about before.

But then my mother said, "I think, we're somewhere in Germany."

We did not know, whether we had to believe it or not.

In the homeland? In the foreign land?

We didn't expect that Germany still existed! The rest of the world had been lost for us. Again and again, my mother tried to catch German characters through a narrow peephole. Then at last, we arrived in a German city, which was called Eisenach in Thuringia.

Our train stopped. We heard for the first time people speak German. They opened the waggon doors, and all the people rushed out of the waggons like animals. We stood at the station and didn't know what was going to happen. We started shouting for something edible. They called us to order, but that was ignored because of sheer hunger and thirst. Once again, the loudspeaker boomed and we had to line up, so that we could get into big trucks, which were ready for us outside the station area. It took some time for the first trucks to leave. Then came our truck and we felt that something good was coming up to us now.

People spoke our language, and it was difficult for us children to understand them. Everything was so strange to us. We drove through the city and couldn't believe that there were still houses that weren't broken, and all people looked differently than we were used to. Sometime later, we entered a forest area; it was a bit hilly there. Suddenly, we saw a fenced building and were afraid to be locked up somewhere again. But we were told by the man who was travelling with us, we didn't need to be afraid, we were in Germany, and this was a camp, where we all would be housed with food and drink, but at first we had to be examined, whether there were sick people among us. This explanation had relieved us of our fears, but great mistrust remained. Now we drove into the camp and came to the place, where those who had arrived before us, were gathered. They stood around frightened waiting for what was going to come up. We were all requested to go to a hall. There were women and men waiting for us there. They provided us with food, and for the first time there was hot tea and hot milk for us children. We could choose seats at nicely set tables; it was like Christmas for us. We got a hot meal and were greeted by friendly people. We took everything joyfully and then later we were able to have a thorough wash in a room, where only women and girls were allowed in, it was all separate.

After that we all had to register. Again we were asked, who we were, when we were born, and where we lived before the Russian invasion. When all this was settled, we were divided into barracks and were able to sleep on a folding cot for the first time. My mother was crying with joy and said to me, "Ulla, now we would have a really good night's sleep." Everyone had the most beautiful night that we hadn't had long since. The next morning the women from the camp had to throw us out of the beds, we simply didn't wake up. Everything was so nice and warm around us, the blankets laid over us, and we hadn't had that for a long time.

In the following days after our arrival on 13 October 1948 in Eisenach, we all were thoroughly examined and vaccinated against all sorts of diseases. We had to be retained in quarantine until 26 November 1948, and then transferred further again. The days after our medical inspection were very tense; we weren't allowed to leave the camp because of epidemic danger. The rumours went around, and the people felt locked up again. There wasn't enough food for everyone, and the rations were getting smaller from day to day.

Camp Siebenborn

I told my mother, I would try to get out of the camp. Then I examined the whole fence around it, if there was a loophole somewhere. The following day, I found a breach I could crawl through. Then I went alone down in the city, came to a street, where there were a few shops, went in there and begged for food. People were amazed that I begged. They asked, where I came from. "There is a camp up there on the mountain, and we're all housed there," I answered. "Oh, in Siebenborn Camp, where the prisoners of war were still two weeks ago, they all were then transferred to Friedland." I said that we all came from Lithuania, and we were beggars there. They didn't know anything about Lithuania. In any case, people gave me bread, margarine and some apples. I was very happy about it and made myself back in the camp, the way I came out. I didn't tell anyone about it; that was my secret, only my mother knew it.

I did that every day, I left in the morning and in the afternoon I was back in the camp. Now we had extra food. A few days later, one tradeswoman gave me a nice sweater in light blue and a dark blue skirt as a gift; I thanked her hugging firmly. I was very proud of the beautiful things and wore them with all due respect. Then the day came, when the administration let all women and children come together, and we learned, where we should go after the camp.

My mother and I were assigned to take up abode in Weißbach near Schmölln in Thuringia. Everyone got a ticket for the journey there by train, and the next day we were driven in trucks from our camp in the mountains down to the station. There were already many children with custodians who most probably had to accompany them. The train arrived at the station and we were told where to board. Another woman came to us with three children; they had also to proceed to Weißbach. We had never met before and got acquainted with each other. We children became friends very quickly. It turned out that they also begged in Lithuania and their home had been Allenstein.

Once again, the train set the wheels in motion with people who had nothing but a desire to get somewhere, where they could get a dwelling place for a lengthy period of time. We all were exhausted on the verge of nervous breakdown and just wanted to have peace around us.

Only the bare necessities

A curiosity awoke in us, where were we being taken yet again now. After a few hours our train arrived at the station Schmölln. A man was already waiting for us at the station exit. He said his name, Henkel from Weissbach, and that he was the mayor of the place. He had a horse-drawn carriage there, and now we all had to climb up there, and with horse and cart we went out into the city. There were seven kilometres to Weißbach. It was a small settlement with a church in the middle of it, and also with a village pond in the settlement's centre. First, we drove to the mayor's office. The people were very friendly to us and gave us some cooked meal, for which we were very grateful. He took our travel documents, which we had brought from Eisenach, and then we were distributed among two farms. The woman with her three children was sent to the lower village.

We were housed just with the mayor's neighbours, family Hofer. It was a good middle-class house with a few rooms, and we came to the first floor, where we were assigned a tiny little room with a cot, a small table, two chairs, a small coal-burning stove, and nothing else.

There were a duvet to cover, a pillow and a bed sheet on the bed, then a wash basin to wash, and a bowl to wash the dishes off, two pots, two plates, cutlery, and two cups, so just only the bare necessities for life.

My mother and I felt like two queens after so much misery that we had behind us. The Hofer family came to greet us and wanted to know a lot about us. My mother then told them, where we came from. They couldn't believe that we came from Lithuania. Then they supplied us with food, everything from their own farm. We enjoyed our small room, where we could be all alone and feel like real people; for the first time we could close a door behind us, wash ourselves properly, cook a meal ourselves and sleep properly in a bed for two of us. We felt happy and contented, and didn't complain that there was only one bed for two; we were satisfied with what was there.

The next day we had to go back to the mayor for registration, and then he gave my mother 25 marks to buy groceries for us. There was a cooperative shop in the village, and something could be bought there. It was a totally different world for us, and it took us quite a while to fit in, because we knew nothing but to move freely and wildly through the countryside. We had to listen attentively to the information the people were providing us with. There were food stamps, shoe and clothing coupons, wood and briquette rations. The Bachmann family, who had been settled down opposite to us, had the same problems, but they had got three rooms. Unlike us, they were treated better.

The first few days we didn't dare to go out at all, just squatted around in the room and enjoyed the four walls, with the fear in the neck, someone could fetch us away from here. But then I first looked at the farm of the Hofer family and marvelled at the many animals they had. I hadn't seen that amount anywhere before and immediately offered my help to clear the dung out of the cowshed and put fresh straw in it. The farmer was delighted with that and said to me, "If you want to help us a little bit, you can do it. Then you will also get some food from us." I ran happily to my mother and told her all about it. She then told me, "You certainly won't be able to do it, because next week after a long time you'll have to go to school again, here in Weißbach. The mayor, Mr. Henkel, has told me so, and now I've signed you up for it."

I was really happy about it and at the same time I got a terrible fear. At night, I couldn't sleep at all and was thinking only about the school. We went again to the mayor and asked him to explain everything to us about the school. Then he gave me a used school bag of his children, a stylus and pencil box. I only had to procure a board for writing. He cheered me up and I lost fear of the first school day. I said to my mother that she had to take me to school, because surely all children would look at me and may notice that I am afraid of it. The children of Mrs. Bachmann had to go there, too. They said to me, "Ulla, if children would want to beat us, then we all must help each other and speak only Lithuanian or Russian. Then they cannot understand what we mean." We swore this for ever and ever.

Until then, I helped the whole day in the stable and was very happy about it, and the houseowners were satisfied with my work. In the evening, they gave me a litre of milk and some sugar beet syrup and some slices of bread to add to it. I went joyfully to my mother with it, and then we sat homely at our little table and felt very comfortable. The small stove that stood in the room was also nice warm. We had got some fire wood and briquettes from the mayor, but then the next ration had to be taken against coal ration coupons in the city of Schmölln, seven kilometres away, at the coal store. But we didn't have a vehicle for that; we had to get a handcart first. The farmer Hofer could have done it with a horse-drawn carriage, but now and then he didn't do that for us, poor people.

I wanted to make friends with his daughter Gerda and son Günther. They were about my age, but seemingly they didn't want that with me, such a poor beggar. I couldn't understand why they were so hostile to me. I talked to my mother about it, and she said to me, "Please, keep away from them. They are rich and we're nothing for them. They don't want to do anything with us. They don't even say hello when they meet me in the stairwell."

I was so sad about that and didn't go in the stable to help anymore. They asked me, why I didn't want to help anymore. I told them, because they were not greeting us, and that they would for sure throw us out of the room soon, and we were very much afraid of that. The farmer Hofer promised me that it wouldn't be so. In any case, we rented the room and needed to pay 20 marks rent every month from now on. He would go to my mother and make a rental contract. So he did, and my mother said to me, "Please, where are we supposed to get the money from?"

I didn't know what money was, I hadn't seen it for so long. My mother began to think about what we should do hereafter.

Comeback

I had to go to school. At the age of 13, I felt like a first-grader. My mother brought me there on the first day; teacher King and school rector Huke were already waiting for me there. The Bachmann children were also present. We were totally scared and dared not to say a word. Teacher King took me into his class. There were children almost as old as me. Everyone looked at me. It was quiet in the class. The teacher assigned me a seat next to a girl, and I sat down there. All my bones were shaking with fear. I will never forget that feeling. Then the teacher said, "So, now come to me and write on the blackboard for us your complete name, so that we know who you are and where you come from." I went to the blackboard, took a piece of chalk and wanted to write, but I could not. I didn't remember how it was written. I stood there as if rooted to the spot and started crying out of sheer shame. The children began to laugh loudly, the teacher exclaimed "Be quiet now!". But they didn't stop. An outrageous fury came up inside me, and I swore myself, "Wait a bit, I'll show it to you some day" and ran out of the door.

I stopped outside in the hallway and had a good cry. Teacher König came to me, gently took my arm and went with me to school rector Huke, told him what had happened, and he railed against the pupils. Then he went down to the class, told all the pupils what I had behind me and that everyone should sympathize with me. They all apologized and I went back to my seat. But I couldn't do anything, because I was dead scared. The teacher König knew the mayor and learned about my past from him. He then told it all the pupils in the fifth grade, so that they were in the know about me.

At home, I told my mother what had happened in class, and she was also very sad about the whole thing. I just couldn't get over it, kept on crying and didn't want to go to school anymore. But the next day, I went back and simply didn't dare to enter the class. It wasn't until the teacher König appeared and he took me with him. I thought that during the whole time in Lithuania as a beggar, no one had been as cruel to me as the children from this village – I was very unhappy in that environment. The teacher noticed all this and then told me he would ask a girl by the name of Margitta Gabler to help me with my homework. I was very happy about that and she said to me, "I also live in Oberdorf, and you can come to me every day in the afternoon, then we both do the homework together." From then on, I went there every day to her, and I regained my courage to learn everything. It was damn hard for me, but I fought my way through it. I, at the age of 13, wanted at least to learn reading, writing, and arithmetic. My mother didn't accept me with my school worries; I didn't need to ask her about anything, I always had to ask others. I was so obsessed now with my study that I used to sit in bed at night reading through the schoolbook and didn't mind that my mother lay next to me and slept soundly. The self-preservation instinct arose in me once again.

Besides the school, I also had to work with the Hofer family in the stable and on the field, so that I could get a little bit of milk, bread, lard or syrup in the evening. My mother had no money and now she had to get a job with a farmer in the village. At that time, there were many farmhouses that were quite large; there was also a large estate with a beautiful pond and an island right in the middle, where ducks and swans were on it. Mother started working for the Wiesner family, where she got some money. Once a month we got the ration cards, and then we needed some money as well to buy the necessary things. There was a place in Schmölln that gave second-hand things to poor people who had nothing. We got coats, dresses, some underwear for both of us and were very happy about it.

So slowly, optimism came back to us, because there was a completely different world around us. Now we knew the year, months, weeks, days and times of the day again. We were again the people who obviously had to assert themselves here. The people kept on saying 'the people from the East' or 'the refugees'. We were homeland expellees, beggar children and late home comers.

Search Service Munich: ,Herbert Wedigkeit is searvching for his parents.'

After some time, I came back to our rector Mr. Huke to get help for the school; he had turned on his radio, which was in the kitchen. His wife always heard the search service from the Red Cross Munich. That was always transmitted at eleven o'clock in the morning. Refugees were looking for their relatives, parents for their children and children for their parents, and I suddenly heard the name "Herbert Wedigkeit is looking for his parents. "I sprang out of the chair with lightning speed, ran into the kitchen to Mrs. Huke and shouted, "Mrs. Huke, Mrs. Huke! This is my brother Herbert. That's his name. I have to run to my mother very quickly. I'm going crazy! My brother Herbert lives!" and I ran as fast as I could to my mother, and raced up the stairs, yanked the door open, and shouted, "Mum, mum! Our Herbert lives! I've just heard it on the radio. He's looking for his mother and father. I haven't misheard. It's true, Mum!" I think I had a shock of joy. I kept on reperting it until my mother said, "Ulla, stop it. That can't be true. They're all no longer alive." – "It's true, mum! Come on, we'll go straight to the Huke family. They've heard it, too."

We went to them and they confirmed it to my mother. Only then, we both did fall into each other's arms and couldn't believe it was true. Mrs. Huke gave us the address of the Search Service Munich. We thanked for the help and ran home quickly. I decided to contact the search service immediately and ask, if it was really our Herbert. I went to Grandma Hofer, and told her that joyful news. She simply didn't know, whether to believe it or not. Then I ran to Inge and told about it everyone I knew. A feeling of happiness without end was in me.

Inge's mother gave me writing paper and also a stamp. I ran to my mother and said, "Mum, I'll write to Munich right now, and next week we'll have the answer if it's true." I was so excited about it and didn't know how to write it. After a while, I managed it anyhow, and then on the same day I brought the letter on foot to the post office in Schmölln. It was just, as if I was carrying a lump of gold. Overwhelmed with joy, I returned to Weißbach and went to the Huke family, thanked them again for teaching me and that I heard it by chance on their radio. If I hadn't been there, none of us would have heard that, because we didn't have a radio.

When I came back to my mother, we both sat in bed and, being happy about the news, embraced each other and cried for joy. I simply couldn't realize it. The next day it was the talk of the day in the whole village. The Huke family had told many people about what had happened in their house. My mother and I could think of nothing else and hoped to get a message from Munich soon.

Many people in the village asked us again and again, if we already had any news from the search service. It was difficult for me to learn at school, because my thoughts were always with Herbert. For me, he had been dead for years. Why was the name on the radio? I wasn't able to understand the whole situation anymore and couldn't apprehend and come to terms with what had happened. It was very bad for me. Mother said almost nothing and sat motionless on our bed. I always asked her, "Mum, is it true that our Herbert lives?" – "I don't know, Ulla."

I think four weeks had passed, and then came the much longed-for letter from Munich confirming that it was about our Herbert. I cried out with joy, and both of us were lucky to have found someone from our family. We read the letter again and again. There it was in black and white that our Herbert had lived since 1947 in Berlin with Uncle Alwi who is the brother of my mother, and we had to contact him. His address was in the letter, and now it was really true. I had to wait for the meeting with another sibling of mine and couldn't believe it. I thought of Aunt Lise in Lithuania, if she hadn't told us the whole truth about my siblings? Well, first I wrote to Uncle Alwin, because they didn't know that we had been already here.

I doubted the whole thing and suddenly got very scared again, if it wasn't yet my brother Herbert and I was happy in vain to have again my brother at last. I was torn over all this. Just as happy, I brought the letter to Uncle Alwin to the post office in Schmölln and was looking forward to the answer that would come. My mother was very sad and spoke little about the whole thing. I don't know why. She often went to Frau Bachmann and came back after hours. Mrs Bachmann told me then that mother cried very often.

After about two weeks, the post came from Berlin. Full of curiosity, I opened the letter and it confirmed the truth: We had found our Herbert again. In 1947, Herbert was brought from Königsberg by the Russians to Berlin-Dahlem as a child ill with tuberculosis. He was found by a Russian nurse nearly dead on the street in Königsberg and taken to hospital. He got then a legal guardian from the Berlin authority, and they might have handed all the matters over to the Search Service Munich, very fortunately for us all. We believed it so, but everything turned out to be different.

The big problem for us was that we had no money at all to go to Berlin. Then I said to my mother, we had to go to the mayor Mr. Henkel. He could certainly give us some help. My thought was the right one.

Mother drove alone and I was once again on my own and inwardly quite empty. But the kids in the school encouraged me. My friend Inge asked me every day: "Ulla, have you heard anything from your mother?" The answer was every day, "No." She stayed away for over a week, and then she reappeared in Weissbach.

In a jovial mood and curious, I was expecting the news my mother had brought from Berlin. But she was very bad-tempered and let fly at once. I got totally scared. "Mum, what happened at Uncle Alwin," I wanted to know, "and why haven't you brought Herbert with you?" The world suddenly collapsed for me again, because I had been so eagerly looking forward to meeting my brother Herbert and now that again. "Ulla," said my mother, "we won't be able to have Herbert back in our family. I couldn't do anything with it." – "Mum, have you seen Herbert?" I asked hopefully. "Yes, I saw him with Uncle Alwin, but he doesn't want to have anything with me. He is now 13 years old and can decide for himself where he wants to grow up and stay. He said he would jump out of the train, if he would have to go back to where the Russians are. He said in a firm voice that he wants to stay with Uncle Alwin forever, and with that he had rejected me as a mother for ever."

It was hard for me to believe that I had lost my brother again. My inner life was as if broken and I was only crying. My mother, on the other hand, was like a mummy. She didn't make any movement at all. She sat staring into space.

"Mum, why don't I have my brother again?" I kept on asking. The answer was, "I do not know."

Epilogue – What happened next...

At first, I couldn't get rid of the thoughts about the bygone difficult years. All my thoughts always went back to Königsberg and Lithuania. It was very hard for me to come over everything. I couldn't enjoy the games of other children. But I found a good girl friend and also school rector Huke continued to help me.

Our relations with the Hofer family were getting worse and worse. We were poor as dirt, but their shelves were full, they didn't lack anything, but we had nothing of it. As the confirmation day came closer, I needed a dress. I could procure it only in the second-hand clothing store. But I was proud anyway. But I was sad, too. All the confirmands came with many relatives and I had no one, not even the father with me.

Soon I had to finish school and got the first testimonial in my life. I wrote about it to my aunt Agnes who lived in Bielefeld in the western zone. She was very happy about my success and sent a big package.

At the age of 14, I had to do an apprenticeship. I wanted to become a tailor, but nothing could be done there. But I could become a button maker in Schmölln, I was told. I did that and learned everything, even if it was hard. But I wanted to get a good qualification, so that I could earn some money.

I got along worse and worse with my mother. We quarrelled and mother was very dissatisfied with everyday life. It was especially bad during Christmas. We had nothing, just apples that were very delicious and red.

I made friends with some other people and discovered my love for sports. I especially liked athletics. I also participated in competitions. One day, I had to go to Berlin and I immediately thought of my brother Herbert.

When we both met again we lay in each other's arms and wept. It was so difficult to come over everything. But then, we calmed down and told each other about our experiences.

Gradually, I grew up. I always learned and my spare time became less. Soon the childhood was completely gone.

I made my own thoughts about the goings-on around me: about the poverty and the mark currency, the Russians who took everything for their own people and the slogans of the new era. I always had to think about Königsberg. At that time – the Hitler Youth marches, now – the songs of the Free German Youth. They sounded almost exactly the same, only the lyrics were different. The youth can be easily made to change its ways.

I realized that everyone was becoming increasingly dissatisfied with the company, where I was working. They could hardly come square with the payments they got and wanted more money. We apprentices didn't comment on that, so that no problems could be caused for us.

Then I looked for a new job, in the household. Mother didn't stop me. But even there I couldn't come to rest. I wanted to go to West-Germany. Others had already succeeded in doing that. I was also determined to do that and there was no way back. I worked out the plan with my mother and didn't tell anyone else. I couldn't even say goodbye.

First, we went to Uncle Alwin in Berlin, but he couldn't keep us long. In the camp Marienfelde we were assigned, where we had to go. We went to Kempen near Krefeld. In March 1954, we arrived there. The mayor of Gefrath picked us up. We came to a shabby barracks; it was plain hell for us. I went straight to the employment office to find something. I did everything. It was bad, when people called me, "These are the Russians or Poles." That was a great humiliation for me.

We didn't get any help, just a refugee card, but it said that I was not entitled to claim anything.

I started then looking for a sports group again. I was even allowed to train a children's group. The little ones were all very excited. I became convinced that I got everything right.

My relations with mother were bad. She yelled at me once,

"Why did I put you in the world, if you don't work for us?" My world crashed after hearing that.

I also found work in the household again, but I received little. I felt like a slave. Only my sport helped me to come over it. Thanks to it, I discovered the life I had never seen before and realized that it started to do good to me and to my soul.

I didn't have a friend. My experiences in Königsberg had filled me with horror. Then an acquaintance of my boss came to see me at my working place. He had a son Klaus whom he also brought with. The young man gave me a smile and our eyes intertwined. It was like we had known each other for ages. His fate was also very sad. We met again and again and soon he didn't want anymore that I got broken because of my work.

We decided to marry on 4 October 1958. Our healthy boy, the little Klaus, was born in 1959. From then on, I had two Klauslings!

Ursula with her sister Eva in Königsberg (around 1943)

Mother's parents, grandmother and grandfather
Hauke in Königsberg (before 1939)

Gerda (cousin) with Hans and Eva
in Königsberg (around 1941)

Aunt Agnes as a young woman
in Königsberg (around 1942)

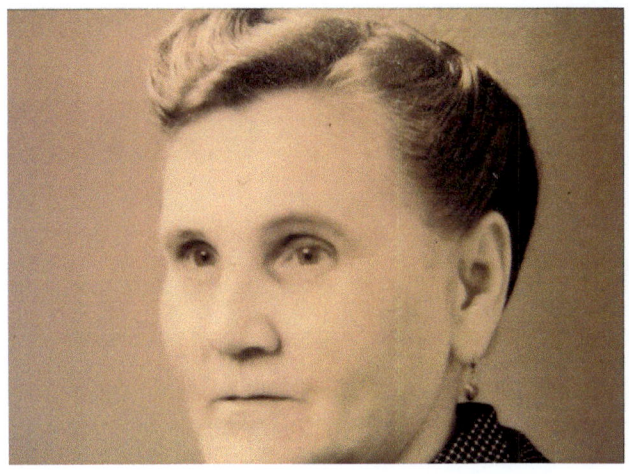

mother in the GDR (after 1945)

School picture in Weißbach / Schmölln, GDR; Ursula in the middle, top row, in a light pullover (Spring 1949)

Uncle Alwin with daughter Gerda and her son Eric in Paris (around 1950)

Ursula in the GDR (1951)

Ursula after fleeing to the Federal Republic of Germany (1954)

The author Ursula Dorn (2007)

The burden of memory

A Commentary by PD Dr. Winfrid Halder

I.

No, this book is not a literary masterpiece. One senses in almost every line that the author does not count among those to whom writing is a common occupation. It is unmistakable that the book was born anything but easy. Of course, this is not because the author sought to realize a certain artistic claim, but because she had to wrestle the letter as such.

Not a literary masterpiece: But precisely this makes the strength of Ursula Dorn's memories peculiar. With a stupendous immediacy, they visualize the experience and sensory world of a ten-year-old over sixty years ago, which could have only been spoiled by artistic sophistication, by literary "pretensions" of whatever kind. The experiences of the child from the final phase of the Second World War and the first post-war period meet the reader almost completely "intellectually unfiltered" – and exactly therefore so deeply.

They have existed long since, the reports of those who predestined by virtue of high education and personal inclination to write put on record the horrors of the demise of the old East Prussia since 1944/45. The books of Hans Graf von Lehndorff (East Prussian diary)[1] and Marion Countess Dönhoff (Names that nobody mentions anymore)[2] are particularly noteworthy here. They rightly belong to the best-known, repeatedly quoted testimonies from this period. Both, in contrast to Ursula Dorn, were already for good measure at the time of the happenings young academically educated adults: the young doctor Lehndorff (born 1910)[3] and the studied economist Dönhoff (born 1909)[4] have themselves experienced terrible things and described them in a way that leaves no reader untouched. At the same time, their testimonies are each shaped by a very specific spiritual-political attitude. A convinced evangelical Christian reveals itself in the case of Lehndorff who stood as a member of the regime-critical "Confessing Church" in unbridgeable distance to the National Socialist tyranny, and saw the downfall of his East Prussian homeland as an inevitable result of the countless and monstrous crimes previously committed in German name in the Soviet Union and elsewhere.[5] Dönhoff shares this undoubtedly correct view; at the same time it was the intention of the countess, who had already matured to become the influential journalist of "Zeit", to underline the irreversibility of the loss of the former eastern territories of the German Reich. Her book "Names that nobody mentions anymore" was first published at the beginning of the 1960s and was met with fierce opposition in the Federal Republic of Germany, not only on the part of the majority of members of the Federation of Expellees.[6]

Nothing like that can be found in the book of Ursula Dorn. It is significant that the name of Hitler is not mentioned at all, the Stalin's one – only incidentally. The lack of a "political background" on the one hand certainly has to do with the origin of the author, who – as they say – comes from "the most ordinary circumstances" and probably never had a whiff of a chance in her live to visit a college, what for Lehndorff and Dönhoff was more or less a matter of course in view of their noble, very well-off parents' houses. However, far more important than the difference in education is likely to have been something else: The memories of Ursula Dorn had been apparently quasi hermetically "encapsulated" for decades; she herself, as it may be assumed, had decidedly avoided touching it. Firstly, this might have been the case due to the fact that for many years it was inopportune and undesirable in the West German public – beyond the marginalized milieu of the Federation of Expellees – to "tell these horror stories again and again". This had to do with a completely misunderstood desire to reconcile with our Eastern European and Eastern European neighbours, with the usually unspoken conviction that understanding was easier to achieve if the acknowledgement of the irrefutable German guilt was accompanied by the concealment of crimes committed against Germans. What a misapprehension.

However, this has changed decisively in recent times: In the culture of remembrance of the Federal Republic of Germany, flight and displacement and their concomitant circumstances in the context of a complex process of change have received a far greater significance in recent years than that had been previously the case for a long time.[7] This has also facilitated the open dialogue on human rights violations against members of the German civilian population.

Beyond the recently changed climate in the public memory discourse, Ursula Dorn's long silence seems to have been induced by another far more decisive factor: self-protection. One doesn't have to be a psychologist to conjecture that by then the twelve-year-old girl could only go on living with the door closed behind such remembrances' background that she had brought to the post-war Germany taking care of it being firmly shut up. This attitude had most probably unburdened her life – and so many others, too – because life (survival), at least in the first decade after 1945, demanded the upmost endeavour from the individual. Beyond that, Dorn lived in the Soviet occupation zone and later in the GDR, where there existed a general, though nowhere open formulated, all the more effective ban on talking about crimes committed by the Soviet "friends"; such a stance was effectively furthered by the East German policymakers.[8]

So Ursula Dorn kept silent until her eighth decade of life. Now she has put her memories on paper - but not really for "the public". The dedication to the son and the granddaughter suggests that the main impulse was to make herself better understood on the part of own neighbours. In any case, other people of similar fate have cited this to legitimize[9] so the revelation of their memories, a revelation that causes the utmost suffering to them and far-off from any drive for self-presentation.

The result is tangibly embodied in a very personal book. The author deserves deep respect for the courage with which she allows outsiders and strangers to share in her painful experiences. The purpose of the book is not voyeurism, but the warning against the abysses of human temptation that succumbs to violence and the consequences that always strike even the most uninvolved. The author deserves the deepest respect, because she has put herself under the burden of memory and made the manuscript that might have without doubt enervated her physically and a good deal more mentally, if not easier but nonetheless more bearable.

The publisher and the editor deserve recognition for their careful handling of the manuscript: even where the text seems to be at times awkward, they have resisted the temptation to "polish" it and have just left it with its peculiarity. As a result, the formulations have been preserved that have a touching effect, above all, through their completely unaffected directness. For example, when the author, after she has reported gruesome details, comes to the conclusion, "My little soul had got thereby a big crack in life." (p. 30)

II.

The experiences described by Ursula Dorn cover mainly the period between the summer of 1944 and October 1948.

Ursula Dorn was born in 1935 in Königsberg; the city had been then the capital of the Prussian province of East Prussia for several hundred years.[10] With around 370,000 inhabitants, Königsberg was not only by far the largest city in the province, but also ranked among the 20 most important German cities. The East Prussian metropolis remained largely untouched by direct influences of war until about the time Ursula Dorn began her report, thanks to its geographical position.

Then however, the war struck the city straightaway with its terrible force: Dorn recalls somewhat vaguely a major bombing raid; in fact those were two nightly attacks carried out by the Royal Air Force on 26/27. and on 29./30. August 1944. The historic centre of Königsberg, including the castle and the cathedral, were almost completely destroyed, and about 40% of the entire city was reduced to rubble and ashes; around 4,600 inhabitants were killed.[11]

The gun shelling raids of Soviet fighter aircrafts described by Ursula Dorn began some time later. In the meantime Konigsberg had to face a completely different disaster besides the attacks from the air: in mid-October 1944 the advancing units of the Red Army crossed for the first time the border of the German Reich; the German armed forces were unable to stop the onslaught permanently.

Now East Prussia finally no longer benefited from its position as the easternmost province, but rather the need for revenge of the soldiers from the Soviet Union that had been previously invaded by the Germans discharged here almost completely uninhibited; the Soviet leadership under Stalin even temporarily fuelled it.[12] There happened terrible excesses against parts of the civilian population, which had not fled in time, already during the first foray into the area of Gumbinnen (about 100 km east of Königsberg).[13]

Ursula Dorn apparently continues to blame her mother for failing to flee the city in good time. In retrospect, however, one can hardly blame the mother for hesitating, because on the one hand, of course, she had to keep an eye on a possible place of refuge - and perhaps there was not such a one from her perspective. On the other hand, the Nazi leadership - especially the Nazi Party Gauleiter Erich Koch - assured again and again that Königsberg would be held by all means and it was only a matter of time until the enemy troops would be repulsed from the whole territory of East Prussia. After all, the party authorities in many places explicitly banned the escape for the mass of the civilian population; this was also applied to Königsberg. However, a stealthy escape movement, evading the official prohibitions (e. g. under the guise of relatives' visits), brought about the situation that at the end of 1944 about 250,000 people still lived in the city.[14]

How completely illusory was the assumption that the Red Army could still be stopped may have become clear to many only after the beginning of the Soviet's final winter offensive in mid-January 1945. Within a few days, the largest part of East Prussia with Königsberg was cut off from the rest of the Reich territory, as Soviet units had advanced to the Baltic Sea in a major envelopment operation at Elbing (about 100 kilometres southwest of Königsberg).

Since January 23, 1945 it had been only possibly to leave the city by way of the port at Pillau and then by sea via the Baltic Sea or even taking a more dangerous way, namely by crossing the frozen Frisches Haff (so mostly on foot over the ice of the Baltic Sea lagoon southwest of Königsberg). Nevertheless, tens of thousands of inhabitants made a desperate attempt to escape from the city. As the Soviet troops quickly tightened the siege ring around the city – on January 27 it had been declared a "fortress" – these opportunities did not exist anymore soon afterwards. The city commandant general Lasch, true to Hitler's orders, had defended Königsberg by all available means until April 9, 1945 despite the fact that there were still approximately 120,000 civilians staying in the city.[15] Consequently, as Ursula Dorn describes it, the remaining population witnessed the murderous battles for the city, which caused countless casualties as a result of the artillery bombardment, firearms' shelling and further devastation. Meanwhile, Erich Koch had long since set off to the west.[16]

General Lasch capitulated with his soldiers only on April 9, 1945; at that time the advancing mass of the Red Army had bypassed Konigsberg and was already standing along the Oder, ready for the last attack on Berlin. Therefore, the military resistance in the city had become completely meaningless.[17] When the Soviet soldiers invaded the remnants of the East Prussian capitals, terrible excesses took place again affecting all the people who had been found there, no matter whether they were wounded soldiers, old men, women or children.

Ursula Dorn tried to describe the indescribable. It's also the fact that she witnessed a seemingly aimless expulsion of the inhabitants from the city who had survived the ordeal for the time being; that death march lasted several weeks. It is still unclear what the victors actually meant by forcing tens of thousands to leave Königsberg before bringing them later back to the field of rubble that had remained from the city; systematic arson had almost completed the work of destruction.[18]

According to Soviet sources, on September 1, 1945 just over 68,000 people[19] lived in Königsberg including barely capable adult men. For the mass of the remaining women and children of German nationality, there was no regulated supply of food and other necessary goods such as medicines. Unlike in the Soviet occupation zone at the same time farther west, the victorious power did not maintain the existing rationing system, but left the remaining population of the city and East Prussia to its own devices in the chaos of destruction that existed everywhere - except thousands, especially women who were downright en masse taken captive in the streets and committed to work without any consideration.

The fear of Ursula Dorn's mother of being committed to forced labour was anything but unfounded. The workforce was used more or less locally largely in agriculture, which was initiated by the winners primarily to supply their own troops, but in a drastically reduced extent compared to the previous period. However, a large number of German workers were also deported to the Soviet Union.[20]

The way of dealing with the rest of the civilian population was presumably conditioned by certain indecisiveness of the Soviet leadership on how to deal with it in the future. It had been admittedly already clear since the Potsdam Conference of the allied major victorious powers (July 17 – August 2, 1945) that the northern part of the former province of East Prussia, including Königsberg, would be transferred to the USSR.[21] Whether the remains of the German population would be left there remained, however, unclear for the time being. Insofar, the terrible time of ubiquitous hunger described by Ursula Dorn falls into the short phase of the immediate post-war period, in which there was still no systematic expulsion from the Soviet-occupied part of East Prussia. On the other hand, there existed virtually no possibility to move legally westwards toward the occupied rest of Germany.

Faced with the imminent threat of starvation, many people tried – as Ursula Dorn and her mother did – to get to Lithuania, hoping to have better chances of survival there. The Lithuanian city of Kaunas, into which Ursula Dorn initially arrived more or less by chance, is situated about 220 kilometres northeast of Königsberg. The term "wolf kids" was born, because there were many children and adolescents among the refugees who had lost their parents during the war.[22]

As a matter of fact, the agricultural conditions and thus the general supply situation in Lithuania were more favourable than in neighbouring East Prussia at that time. Although the war had also hit this country, there had not been such a disastrous amount of devastation there. The Lithuanian population remained largely at their homes, even after the German Wehrmacht had abandoned the land and the Red Army moved in. As a result, the agricultural structures remained largely intact. This enabled the Lithuanians to help the German children and adults who wandered about begging a meal; and, as Ursula Dorn describes, were often ready to do that.

At the same time, Lithuania was anything but a haven of peace and security in the post-war era, which is also clear from Dorn's report. After a century and a half of belonging to the Russian Empire, the country gained its independence as a result of the First World War. However, this was lost again in 1940: the Hitler-Stalin Pact of August 1939 assigned Lithuania to the Soviet sphere of influence; then the country was occupied by the Red Army in 1940 and annexed to the USSR. The Stalinist regime took ruthless action mainly against the Lithuanian elites. Then, in the course of the attack on the Soviet Union, the German Wehrmacht occupied Lithuania in the summer of 1941 and established an occupation regime, which was not inferior to Soviet brutality. The Red Army returned in 1944 to re-establish the "Lithuanian Soviet Socialist Republic". Once again, an arbitrary rule was brought about, which proceeded ruthless against all actual or alleged independence efforts undertaken by the Lithuanian side.[23]

Ursula Dorn reports on the fear of the population for the arrests made by the Soviet secret service. Tens of thousands of Lithuanians were deported to the Soviet penal system at that time; thousands of others were forced to go into exile. Until about the mid-1950s, there was also armed resistance from the Lithuanian side against the Stalinist regime. However, this was broken using massive military means.[24] The fact that Ursula Dorn and many others received help from Lithuanian people can hardly be overestimated.

Because these helpers knew that they endangered themselves to a high degree, if they assisted the persecuted Germans. These deserts should not be belittled due to the fact that this help was not always granted disinterested and the homeless were occasionally used as cheap labour.

The fact that Ursula Dorn and her mother not only survived, but even after they had finally been picked up by Soviet soldiers, arrived in a rail transport with other Germans of East Prussian origin to Thuringia, seems to be almost a miracle. The USSR leadership had decided by then to drive the remaining German population out of the part of East Prussia that had been fallen to it completely. In July 1946, Königsberg was renamed Kaliningrad to underline its future permanent affiliation with the USSR. The famine – in the course of which there were even cases of cannibalism – and the associated epidemic diseases had cost the lives of some 100,000 people.

In 1947/48, about 25,000 surviving inhabitants of Königsberg arrived with the transports organized by the Soviet side in the Soviet or one of the three western occupation zones in the rest of Germany[25]. Ursula Dorn and her mother might have come with one of the last transports.

Winfrid Halder

PD Dr. Winfrid Halder was born in 1962 in Dinslaken (North Rhine-Westphalia) and grew up in Upper Bavaria. In 1984–1992, he studied history and political science in Munich and in Freiburg im Breisgau. After Magister Artium (1989) and Ph.D. (1992), he was a research assistant and senior assistant at the Department of Economic and Cultural History of the TU Dresden in 1993–2003. Since 2006, Winfrid Halder has been Director of the Gerhart Hauptmann-Haus Foundation in Dusseldorf and since 2008 – adjunct professor at Heinrich Heine University of Düsseldorf.

Contact:
Stiftung Gerhart-Hauptmann-Haus
Deutsch-osteuropäisches Forum
Bismarckstraße 90
40210 Düsseldorf • Deutschland
Tel. +49 (0)211 / 16 991-12 or -14
Fax +49 (0)211 / 353 118
E-Mail: halder@g-h-h.de
Website: www.g-h-h.de

Explanatory notes

1. cf. Lehndorff, Hans Graf von: Ostpreußisches Tagebuch. Aufzeichnungen eines Arztes aus den Jahren 1945–1947, München 1961.
2. cf. Dönhoff, Marion Gräfin von: Namen, die keiner mehr nennt. Ostpreußen – Menschen und Geschichte, Düsseldorf 1962 [since then numerous editions].
3. cf. Kock, Erich: Chronist des „nüchternen Mundes", in: Die politische Meinung Nr. 366/Mai 2000, pp. 74–76; p. 74.
4. cf. Kuenheim, Haug von: Marion Dönhoff, 4. edition, Reinbek bei Hamburg 2003, p. 8 ff.
5. cf. Kock, Chronist, p. 75.
6. cf. Kuenheim, Dönhoff, p. 94 ff.
7. cf. Hirsch, Helga: Flucht und Vertreibung. Kollektive Erinnerung im Wandel, in: Aus Politik und Zeitgeschichte B 40/41/2003, pp. 14–26; p. 14 ff.
8. cf. Schwartz, Michael: Der historische deutsche Osten in der Erinnerungskultur der DDR, in: Gauger, Jörg-Dieter/ Kittel, Manfred (ed.): Die Vertreibung der Deutschen in der Erinnerungskultur, St. Augustin 2005, p. 69–84; p. 69 ff.
9. cf. e.g. Sumowski, Hans-Burkhard: „Jetzt war ich ganz allein auf der Welt". Erinnerungen an eine Kindheit in Königsberg 1944–1947, München 2007, p. 7 ff.
10. cf. Manthey, Jürgen: Königsberg. Geschichte einer Weltbürgerrepublik, München 2006 [TB-edition], p. 16 ff.
11. cf. Manthey, Königsberg, p. 667.
12. cf. Halder, Winfrid: Im Teufelskreis der Gewalt. Sowjetische Soldaten und deutsche Zivilbevölkerung 1944/45. Anmerkungen zu neueren Forschungsergebnissen, in:

Deutschland-Archiv 5/2007, pp. 815–823; p. 815 ff.

13. cf. Franzen, K. Erik: Die Vertriebenen. Hitlers letzte Opfer, München 2002 [TB-edition], p. 40 f.
14. cf. Franzen, Vertriebene, p. 81 ff.
15. cf. Manthey, Königsberg, p. 669 ff.
16. cf. Knopp, Guido/Tewes, Annette: Die Eingeschlossenen, in: Knopp, Guido: Der Sturm. Kriegsende im Osten, München 2004, pp. 68–117; p. 68 ff.
17. cf. Zeidler, Manfred: Kriegsende im Osten. Die Rote Armee und die Besetzung Deutschlands östlich von Oder und Neiße, München 1996, bes. p. 83 ff.
18. cf. Manthey, Königsberg, p. 671 f.
19. cf. Kibelka, Ruth: Ostpreußens Schicksalsjahre 1944–1948, Berlin 2004, p. 46.
20. cf. Franzen, Vertriebene, p. 91 ff.
21. cf. Benz, Wolfgang: Potsdam 1945. Besatzungsherrschaft und Neuaufbau im Vier-Zonen-Deutschland, 3. Aufl., München 1994, S. 93 ff.
22. cf. Kibelka, Ruth: Wolfskinder. Grenzgänger an der Memel, Berlin 1996, bes. S. 81 ff.
23. cf. Butenschön, Marianna: Litauen, München 2002, S. 94 ff.
24. cf. Butenschön, Litauen, S. 102 ff.
25. cf. Manthey, Königsberg, S. 673 ff.

Bibliografische Information der Deutschen Natinalbibliothek:
Die Deutsche Nationalbibliothek verzeichnet diese Publikation
in der Deutsche Nationalbibliografie; detaillierte bibliografische
Daten sind im Internet über http:// dnb.dnb.de abrufbar

Englische Übersetzung:
© Ausbildungs- und Forschungszentrum ETHNOS e. V. 2019

Bezugsadresse:
AFZ ETHNOS, Bermesdickerstr. 9, 44357 Dortmund

Herstellung:
BoD – Books on Demand, Norderstedt

ISBN 978-3-74-942920-2